More Strawberries

© Nelson Canada,
A Division of International Thomson Limited, 1990

Published in 1990 by
Nelson Canada,
A Division of International Thomson Limited
1120 Birchmount Road
Scarborough, Ontario M1K 5G4

ISBN 0-17-603044-1
Teacher's Guide 0-17-603045-X

Editors: Joseph S. Banel, James A. MacNeill, Glen A. Sorestad
Project Manager: Lana Kong
In-house Editor: Linda Bishop
Art Director: Lorraine Tuson
Designer: Tracy Walker
Cover Design: Tracy Walker
Cover Illustration: Nicholas Vitacco
Photo Research: Jane Affleck

Nelson Canada also wishes to thank Gail C. Roberts,
English Language Arts Co-ordinator of
the St. James-Assiniboia School Division,
for her continuing contributions to this project.

Printed and bound in Canada

4567890/   /987654

Canadian Cataloguing in Publication Data

Main entry under title:
More strawberries

ISBN 0-17-603044-1

1. Children's stories. 2. Children's stories,
Canadian (English).* 3. Short stories. 4. Short
stories, Canadian (English).* I. Banel, Joseph, 1943—

PZ5.M67 1990   j808.83'1   C89-095174-8

More Strawberries

REFLECTIONS IN FICTION

JOSEPH S. BANEL

JAMES A. MᴀᴄNEILL

GLEN A. SORESTAD

Nelson Canada

CONTENTS

STRANGE TALES

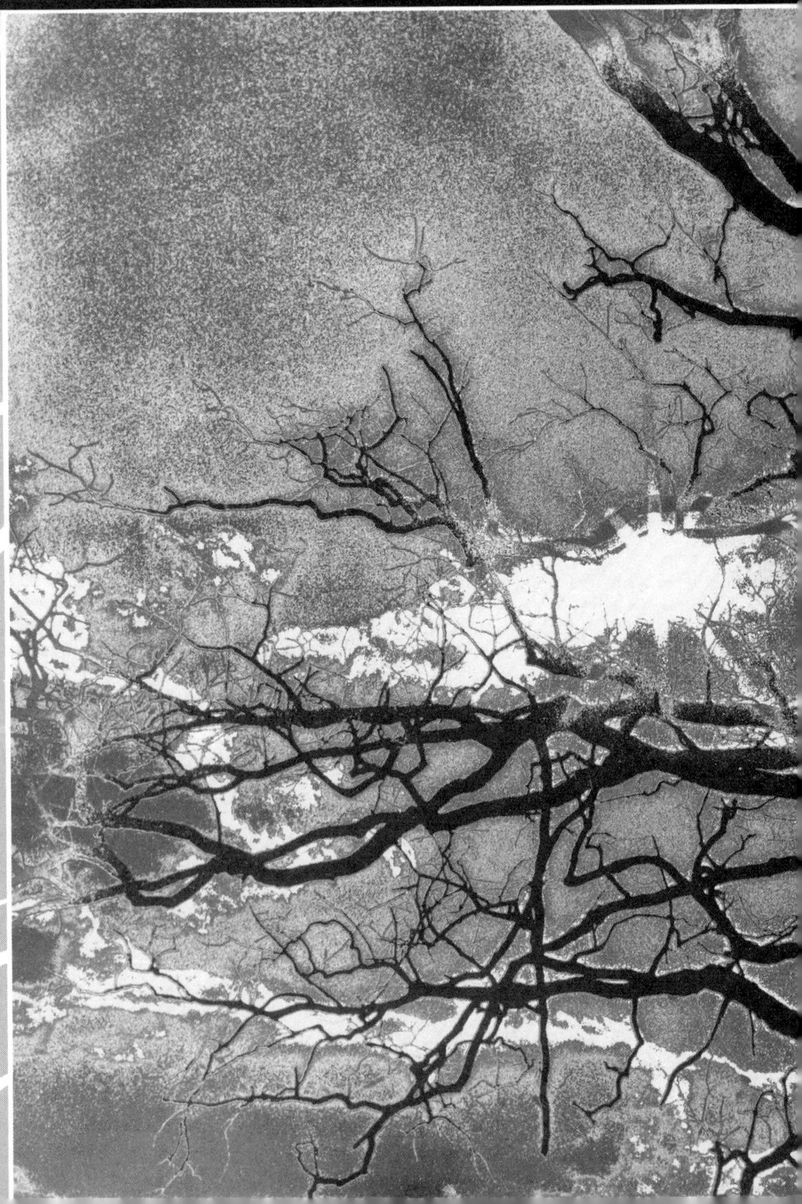

Future Tense

BY ROBERT
LIPSYTE

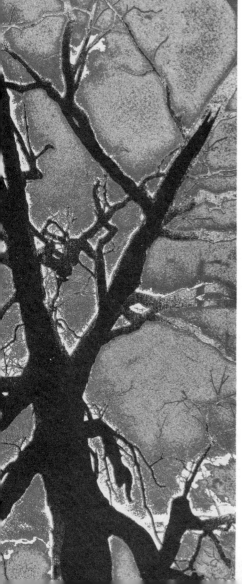

Cold sweat covered Gary's body as Mr. Smith grabbed his arm and led him to the new vice-principal. Gary got a good look at her for the first time. He blurted, "Are you going to enlist me or erase me?"

Gary couldn't wait for tenth grade to start so he could strut his sentences, parade his paragraphs, renew his reputation as the top creative writer in school. At the opening assembly, he felt on edge, psyched, like a boxer before the first-round bell. He leaned forward as Dr. Proctor, the principal, introduced two new staff members. He wasn't particularly interested in the new vice-principal, Ms. Jones; Gary never had discipline problems, he'd never even had to stay after school. But his head cocked alertly

7

as Dr. Proctor introduced the new Honours English teacher, Mr. Smith. Here was the person he'd have to impress.

He studied Mr. Smith. The man was hard to describe. He looked as though he'd been manufactured to fit his name. Average height, brownish hair, pale white skin, medium build. Middle age. He was the sort of person you began to forget the minute you met him. Even his clothes had no particular style. They merely covered his body.

Mr. Smith was. . .just there.

Gary was studying Mr. Smith so intently that he didn't hear Dr. Proctor call him up to the stage to receive an award from last term. Jim Baggs jabbed an elbow into his ribs and said, "Let's get up there, Dude."

Dr. Proctor shook Gary's hand and gave him the County Medal for Best Composition. While Dr. Proctor was giving Jim Baggs the County Trophy for Best All-Round Athlete, Gary glanced over his shoulder to see if Mr. Smith was so ordinary he was invisible when no one was talking about him.

On the way home, Dani Belzer, the prettiest poet in school, asked Gary, "What did you think of our new Mr. Wordsmith?"

"If he was a colour he'd be beige," said Gary. "If he was a taste he'd be water. If he was a sound he'd be a low hum."

"Fancy, empty words," sneered Mike Chung, ace reporter on the school paper. "All you've told me is you've got nothing to tell me."

Dani quickly stepped between them. "What did you think of the first assignment?"

"Describe a Typical Day at School," said Gary, trying unsuccessfully to mimic Mr. Smith's bland voice. "That's about as exciting as tofu."

"A real artist," said Dani, "accepts the commonplace as a challenge."

That night, hunched over his humming electric typewriter, Gary wrote a description of a typical day at school from the viewpoint of a new teacher who was seeing everything for the first time, who took nothing for granted. He described the shredded edges of the limp flag outside the dented front door, the worn flooring where generations of kids had nervously paced outside the principal's office, the nauseatingly sweet pipe-smoke seeping out of the teachers' lounge.

And then, in the last line, he gave the composition that extra twist, the little kicker on which his reputation rested. He wrote:

The new teacher's beady little eyes missed nothing, for they were the optical recorders of an alien creature who had come to earth to gather information.

The next morning, when Mr. Smith asked for a volunteer to read aloud, Gary was on his feet and moving toward the front of the classroom before Mike Chung got his hand out of his pocket.

The class loved Gary's composition. They laughed and stamped their feet. Chung shrugged, which meant he couldn't think of any criticism, and Dani flashed thumbs up. Best of all, Jim Baggs shouldered Gary against the blackboard after class and said, "Awesome tale, Dude."

Gary felt good until he got the composition back. Along the margin, in perfect script, Mr. Smith had written:

You can do better.

"How would he know?" Gary complained on the way home.

"You should be grateful," said Dani. "He's pushing you to the farthest limits of your talent."

"Which may be nearer than you think," snickered Mike.

Gary rewrote his composition, expanded it, complicated it, thickened it. Not only was this new teacher an alien, he was part of an extraterrestrial conspiracy to take over Earth. Gary's final sentence was:

Every iota of information, fragment of fact, morsel of minutiae sucked up by those vacuuming eyes was beamed directly into a computer circling the planet. The data would eventually become a program that would control the mind of every school kid on earth.

Gary showed the new draft to Dani before class. He stood on tiptoes so he could read over her shoulder. Sometimes he wished she were shorter, but mostly he wished he were taller.

"What do you think?"

"The assignment was to describe a typical day," said Dani. "This is off the wall."

He snatched the papers back. "Creative writing means creating." He walked away, hurt and angry. He thought: *If she doesn't like my compositions, how can I ever get her to like me?*

That morning, Mike Chung read his own composition aloud to the class. He described a typical day through the eyes of a student in a wheelchair. Everything most students take for granted was an obstacle: the bathroom door too heavy to open, the gym steps too steep to climb, the light switch too high on the wall. The class applauded and Mr. Smith smiled approvingly. Even Gary had to admit it was really good—if you considered plain-fact journalism as creative writing, that is.

Gary's rewrite came back the next day marked:

Improving. Try again.

Saturday he locked himself in his room after breakfast and rewrote the rewrite. He carefully selected his nouns and verbs and adjectives. He polished and arranged them in sentences like a jeweller strings pearls. He felt good as he wrote, as the electric typewriter hummed and buzzed and sometimes coughed. He thought: *Every champion knows that as hard as it is to get to the top, it's even harder to stay up there.*

His mother knocked on his door around noon. When he let her in, she said, "It's a beautiful day."

"Big project," he mumbled. He wanted to avoid a distracting conversation.

She smiled. "If you spend too much time in your room, you'll turn into a mushroom."

He wasn't listening. "Thanks. Anything's okay. Don't forget the mayonnaise."

Gary wrote:

> The alien's probes trembled as he read the student's composition. Could that skinny, bespectacled earthling really suspect its extraterrestrial identity? Or was his composition merely the result of a creative thunderstorm in a brilliant young mind?

Before Gary turned in his composition on Monday morning, he showed it to Mike Chung. He should have known better.

"You're trying too hard," chortled Chung. "Truth is stronger than fiction."

Gary flinched at that. It hurt. It might be true. But he couldn't let his competition know he had scored. "You journalists are stuck in the present and the past," growled Gary. "Imagination prepares us for what's going to happen."

Dani read her composition aloud to the class. It described a typical day from the perspective of a louse choosing a head of hair to nest in. The louse moved from a thicket of a varsity crew-cut to the matted jungle of a sagging perm to a straight, sleek blond cascade.

The class cheered and Mr. Smith smiled. Gary felt a twinge of jealousy. Dani and Mike were coming on. There wasn't room for more than one at the top.

In the hallway, he said to Dani, "And you called my composition off the wall?"

Mike jumped in, "There's a big difference between poetical metaphor and hack science fiction."

Gary felt choked by a lump in his throat. He hurried away.

Mr. Smith handed back Gary's composition the next day marked:

See me after school.

Gary was nervous all day. What was there to talk about? Maybe Mr. Smith hated science fiction. One of those traditional English teachers. Didn't understand that science fiction could be literature. *Maybe I can educate him,* thought Gary.

When Gary arrived at the English office, Mr. Smith seemed nervous too. He kept folding and unfolding Gary's composition. "Where do you get such ideas?" he asked in his monotone voice.

Gary shrugged. "They just come to me."

"Alien teachers. Taking over the minds of schoolchildren." Mr. Smith's empty eyes were blinking. "What made you think of that?"

"I've always had this vivid imagination."

Mr. Smith looked relieved. "I guess everything will work out." He handed back Gary's composition. "No more fantasy, Gary. Reality. That's your assignment. Write only about what you know."

Outside school, Gary ran into Jim Baggs, who looked surprised to see him. "Don't tell me you had to stay after, Dude."

"I had to see Mr. Smith about my composition. He didn't like it. Told me to stick to reality."

"Don't listen." Jim Baggs body-checked Gary into the schoolyard fence. "Dude, you got to be yourself."

Gary ran all the way home and locked himself into his room. He felt feverish with creativity. Dude, you got to be yourself, Dude. It doesn't matter what your so-called friends say, or your English teacher. You've got to play your own kind of game, write your own kind of stories.

The words flowed out of Gary's mind and through his fingers and out of the machine onto sheets of paper. He wrote and rewrote until he felt the words were exactly right:

> With great effort, the alien shut down the electrical panic impulses coursing through its system and turned on Logical Overdrive. There were two possibilities:
>
> 1. This high school boy was exactly what he seemed to be, a brilliant, imaginative, apprentice best-selling author and screenwriter, or,
>
> 2. He had somehow stumbled onto the secret plan and he would have to be either enlisted into the conspiracy or erased off the face of the planet.

First thing in the morning, Gary turned in his new rewrite to Mr. Smith. A half hour later, Mr. Smith called Gary out of Spanish. There was no expression on his regular features. He said, "I'm going to need some help with you."

Cold sweat covered Gary's body as Mr. Smith grabbed his arm and led him to the new vice-principal. She read the composition while they waited. Gary got a good look at her for the first time. Ms. Jones was. . .just there. She looked as though she'd been manufactured to fit her name. Average. Standard. Typical. The cold sweat turned into goose pimples.

How could he have missed the clues? Smith and Jones were aliens! He had stumbled on their secret and now they'd have to deal with him.

He blurted, "Are you going to enlist me or erase me?"

Ms. Jones ignored him. "In my opinion, Mr. Smith, you are overreacting. This sort of nonsense"—she waved Gary's composition—"is the typical response of an overstimulated adolescent to the mixture of reality and fantasy in an environment dominated by manipulative music, television, and films. Nothing for us to worry about."

"If you're sure, Ms. Jones," said Mr. Smith. He didn't sound sure.

The vice-principal looked at Gary for the first time. There was no expression in her eyes. Her voice was flat. "You'd better get off this science-fiction kick," she said. "If you know what's good for you."

"I'll never tell another human being, I swear," he babbled.

"What are you talking about?" asked Ms. Jones.

"Your secret is safe with me," he lied. He thought, *If I can just get away from them. Alert the authorities. Save the planet.*

"You see," said Ms. Jones, "you're writing yourself into a crazed state."

"You're beginning to believe your own fantasies," said Mr. Smith.

"I'm not going to do anything this time," said Ms. Jones, "but you must promise to write only about what you know."

"Or I'll have to fail you," said Mr. Smith.

"For your own good," said Ms. Jones. "Writing can be very dangerous."

"Especially for writers," said Mr. Smith, "who write about things they shouldn't."

"Absolutely," said Gary, "positively no question about it. Only what I know." He backed out of the door, nodding his head, thinking, *Just a few more steps and I'm okay. I hope these aliens can't read minds.*

Jim Baggs was practicing head fakes in the hallway. He slammed Gary into the wall with a hip block. "How's it going, Dude?" he asked, helping Gary up.

"Aliens," gasped Gary. "Told me no more science fiction."

"They can't treat a star writer like that," said Jim. "See what the head honcho's got to say." He grabbed Gary's wrist and dragged him into the principal's office.

"What can I do for you, boys?" boomed Dr. Proctor.

"They're messing with his moves, Doc," said Jim Baggs. "You got to let the aces run their races."

"Thank you, James." Dr. Proctor popped his forefinger at the door. "I'll handle this."

"You're home free, Dude," said Jim, whacking Gary across the shoulder blades as he left.

"From the beginning," ordered Dr. Proctor. He nodded sympathetically as Gary told the entire story, from the opening assembly to the meeting with Mr. Smith and Ms. Jones. When Gary was finished, Dr. Proctor took the papers from Gary's hand. He shook his head as he read Gary's last rewrite.

"You really have a way with words, Gary. I should have sensed you were on to something."

Gary's stomach flipped. "You really think there could be aliens trying to take over Earth?"

"Certainly," said Dr. Proctor, matter-of-factly. "Earth is the ripest plum in the universe."

Gary wasn't sure if he should feel relieved that he wasn't crazy or be scared out of his mind. He took a deep breath to control the quaver in his voice, and said: "I spotted Smith and Jones right away. They look like they were manufactured to fit their names. Obviously humanoids. Panicked as soon as they knew I was on to them."

Dr. Proctor chuckled and shook his head. "No self-respecting civilization would send those two stiffs to Earth."

"They're not aliens?" He felt relieved and disappointed at the same time.

"I checked them out myself," said Dr. Proctor. "Just two average, standard, typical human beings, with no imagination, no creativity."

"So why'd you hire them?"

Dr. Proctor laughed. "Because they'd never spot an alien. No creative imagination. That's why I got rid of the last vice-principal and the last Honours English teacher. They were giving me odd little glances when they thought I wasn't looking. After ten years on your planet, I've learned to smell trouble."

Gary's spine turned to ice and dripped down the backs of his legs. "You're an alien!"

"Great composition," said Dr. Proctor, waving Gary's papers. "Grammatical, vividly written, and totally accurate."

"It's just a composition," babbled Gary, "made the whole thing up, imagination, you know."

Dr. Proctor removed the face of his wristwatch and began tapping tiny buttons. "Always liked writers. I majored in your planet's literature. Writers are the keepers of the past and the hope of the future. Too bad they cause so much trouble in the present."

"I won't tell anyone," cried Gary. "Your secret's safe with me." He began to back slowly toward the door.

Dr. Proctor shook his head. "How can writers keep secrets, Gary? It's their natures to share their creations with the world." He tapped three times and froze Gary in place, one foot raised to step out the door.

"But it was only a composition," screamed Gary as his body disappeared before his eyes.

"And I can't wait to hear what the folks back home say when you read it to them," said Dr. Proctor.

"I made it all up." Gary had the sensation of rocketing upward. "I made up the whole..."

—◟

What did you think would happen after reading the first two pages? Were you right?

What might happen next?

The Monkey's Paw

BY W.W. JACOBS

"The first man had his three wishes," the sergeant-major replied. "I don't know what the first two were, but the third was for death. That's how I got the paw."

Without, the night was cold and wet, but in the small parlour of Laburnum Villa the blinds were drawn and the fire burned brightly. Father and son were at chess, the former, who possessed ideas about the game involving radical changes, putting his king into such sharp and unnecessary perils that it even provoked comment from the white-haired old lady knitting placidly by the fire.

"Hark at the wind," said Mr. White, who, having seen a fatal mistake after it was too late, was amiably desirous of preventing his son from seeing it.

"I'm listening," said the latter, grimly surveying the board as he stretched out his hand. "Check."

"I should hardly think that he'd come tonight," said his father, with his hand poised over the board.

"Mate," replied the son.

"That's the worst of living so far out," bawled Mr. White, with sudden and unlooked-for violence; "of all the beastly, slushy, out-of-the-way places to live in, this is the worst. Pathway's a bog, and the road's a torrent. I don't know what people are thinking about. I suppose because only two houses in the road are let, they think it doesn't matter."

"Never mind dear," said his wife soothingly; "perhaps you'll win the next one."

Mr. White looked up sharply, just in time to intercept a knowing glance between mother and son. The words died away on his lips, and he hid a guilty grin in his thin grey beard.

"There he is," said Herbert White, as the gate banged loudly, and heavy footsteps came towards the door.

The old man rose with hospitable haste, and opening the door, was heard condoling with the new arrival. The new arrival also condoled with himself, so that Mrs. White said, "Tut, Tut!" and coughed gently as her husband entered the room, followed by a tall, burly man, beady of eye and rubicund of visage.

"Sergeant-Major Morris," he said, introducing him.

The sergeant-major shook hands, and taking the proffered seat by the fire, watched contentedly while his host got out whisky and tumblers and stood a small copper kettle on the fire.

At the third glass his eyes got brighter, and he began to talk, the little family circle regarding with eager interest this visitor from distant parts, as he squared his broad shoulders in the chair and spoke of wild scenes and doughty deeds; of wars and plagues and strange peoples.

"Twenty-one years of it," said Mr. White, nodding at his wife and son. "When he went away he was a slip of a youth in the warehouse. Now look at him."

"He don't look to have taken much harm," said Mrs. White politely.

"I'd like to go to India myself," said the old man, "just to look round a bit, you know."

"Better where you are," said the sergeant-major, shaking his head. He put down the empty glass, and sighing softly, shook it again.

"I should like to see those old temples and fakirs and jugglers," said the old man. "What was that you started telling me the other day about a monkey's paw or something, Morris?"

"Nothing," said the soldier hastily. "Leastways nothing worth hearing."

"Monkey's paw?" said Mrs. White curiously.

"Well, it's just a bit of what you might call magic, perhaps," said the sergeant-major off-handedly.

His three listeners leaned forward eagerly. The visitor absent-mindedly put his empty glass to his lips and then set it down again. His host filled it for him.

"To look at," said the sergeant-major, fumbling in his pocket, "it's just an ordinary little paw, dried to a mummy."

He took something out of his pocket and proffered it. Mrs. White drew back with a grimace, but her son, taking it, examined it curiously.

"And what is there special about it?" inquired Mr. White as he took it from his son, and having examined it, placed it upon the table.

"It had a spell put on it by an old fakir," said the sergeant-major, "a very holy man. He wanted to show that fate ruled people's lives, and that those who interfered with it did so to their sorrow. He put a spell on it so that three separate men could each have three wishes from it."

His manner was so impressive that his hearers were conscious that their light laughter jarred somewhat.

"Well, why don't you have three, sir?" said Herbert White cleverly.

The soldier regarded him in the way that middle age is wont to regard presumptuous youth. "I have," he said quietly, and his blotchy face whitened.

"And did you really have the three wishes granted?" asked Mrs. White.

"I did," said the sergeant-major, and his glass tapped against his strong teeth.

"And has anybody else wished?" persisted the old lady.

"The first man had his three wishes. Yes," was the reply; "I don't know what the first two were, but the third was for death. That's how I got the paw."

His tones were so grave that a hush fell upon the group.

"If you've had your three wishes, it's no good to you now, then, Morris," said the old man at last. "What do you keep it for?"

The soldier shook his head. "Fancy, I suppose," he said slowly. "I did have some idea of selling it, but I don't think I will. It has caused enough mischief already. Besides, people won't buy. They think it's a fairy tale, some of them; and those who do think anything of it want to try it first and pay me afterward."

"If you could have another three wishes," said the old man, eyeing him keenly, "would you have them?"

"I don't know," said the other. "I don't know."

He took the paw, and dangling it between his forefinger and thumb, suddenly threw it upon the fire. White, with a slight cry, stooped down and snatched it off.

"Better let it burn," said the soldier solemnly.

"If you don't want it, Morris," said the other, "give it to me."

"I won't," said his friend doggedly. "I threw it on the fire. If you keep it, don't blame me for what happens. Pitch it on the fire again like a sensible man."

The other shook his head and examined his new possession closely. "How do you do it?" he inquired.

"Hold it up in your right hand and wish aloud," said the sergeant-major, "but I warn you of the consequences."

"Sounds like the Arabian Nights," said Mrs. White, as she rose and began to set the supper. "Don't you think you might wish for four pairs of hands for me?"

Her husband drew the talisman from his pocket, and then all three burst into laughter as the sergeant-major, with a look of alarm on his face, caught him by the arm.

"If you must wish," he said gruffly, "wish for something sensible."

Mr. White dropped it back in his pocket, and placing chairs, motioned his friend to the table. In the business of supper the talisman was partly forgotten, and afterward the three sat listening in an enthralled fashion to a second instalment of the soldier's adventures in India.

"If the tale about the monkey's paw is not more truthful than those he has been telling us," said Herbert, as the door closed behind their guest, just in time for him to catch the last train, "we shan't make much out of it."

"Did you give him anything for it, father?" inquired Mrs. White, regarding her husband closely.

"A trifle," said he, colouring slightly. "He didn't want it, but I made him take it. And he pressed me again to throw it away."

"Likely," said Herbert, with pretended horror. "Why, we're going to be rich, and famous and happy. Wish to be an emperor, father, to begin with; then you can't be henpecked."

He darted round the table, pursued by the maligned Mrs. White armed with an antimacassar.

Mr. White took the paw from his pocket and eyed it dubiously. "I don't know what to wish for, and that's a fact," he said slowly. "It seems to me I've got all I want."

"If you only cleared the house, you'd be quite happy, wouldn't you?" said Herbert, with his hand on his shoulder. "Well, wish for two hundred pounds, then; that'll just do it."

His father, smiling shamefacedly at his own credulity, held up the talisman, as his son, with a solemn face, somewhat marred by a wink at his mother, sat down at the piano and struck a few impressive chords.

"I wish for two hundred pounds," said the old man distinctly.

A fine crash from the piano greeted the words, interrupted by a shuddering cry from the old man. His wife and son ran towards him.

"It moved," he cried, with a glance of disgust at the object as it lay on the floor. "As I wished, it twisted in my hand like a snake."

"Well, I don't see the money," said his son as he picked it up and placed it on the table, "and I bet I never shall."

"It must have been your fancy, father," said his wife, regarding him anxiously.

He shook his head. "Never mind, though; there's no harm done, but it gave me a shock all the same."

They sat down by the fire again while the two men finished their pipes. Outside, the wind was higher than ever, and the old man started nervously at the sound of a door banging upstairs. A silence unusual and depressing settled upon all three, which lasted until the old couple rose to retire for the night.

"I expect you'll find the cash tied up in a big bag in the middle of your bed," said Herbert, as he bade them good night, "and something horrible squatting up on top of the wardrobe watching you as you pocket your ill-gotten gains."

He sat alone in the darkness, gazing at the dying fire, and seeing faces in it. The last face was so horrible and so simian that he gazed at it in amazement. It got so vivid that, with a little uneasy laugh, he felt on the table for a glass containing a little water to throw over it. His hand grasped the monkey's paw, and with a little shiver he wiped his hand on his coat and went up to bed.

In the brightness of the wintry sun next morning as it streamed over the breakfast table he laughed at his fears. There was an air of prosaic wholesomeness about the room which it had lacked on the previous night, and the dirty, shrivelled little paw was pitched on the sideboard with a carelessness which betokened no great belief in its virtues.

"I suppose all old soldiers are the same," said Mrs. White. "The idea of our listening to such nonsense! How could wishes be granted in these days? And if they could, how could two hundred pounds hurt you, father?"

"Might drop on his head from the sky," said the frivolous Herbert.

"Morris said the things happened so naturally," said his father, "That you might if you so wished attribute it to coincidence."

"Well, don't break into the money before I come back," said Herbert as he rose from the table. "I'm afraid it'll turn you into a mean, avaricious man, and we shall have to disown you."

His mother laughed, and following him to the door, watched him down the road; and returning to the breakfast table, was very happy at the expense of her husband's credulity. All of which did not prevent her from scurrying to the door at the postman's knock, nor prevent her from referring somewhat shortly to retired sergeant-majors of bibulous habits when she found that the post brought a tailor's bill.

"Herbert will have some more of his funny remarks, I expect, when he comes home," said the old lady, as they sat at dinner.

"I dare say," said Mr. White, pouring himself out some beer; "but for all that, the thing moved in my hand; that I'll swear to."

"You thought it did," said the old lady soothingly.

"I say it did," replied the other. "There was no thought about it; I had just—What's the matter?"

His wife made no reply. She was watching the mysterious movements of a man outside, who, peering in an undecided fashion at the house, appeared to be trying to make up his mind to enter. In mental connection with the two hundred pounds, she noticed the stranger was well dressed, and wore a silk hat of glossy newness. Three times he paused at the gate, and then walked on again. The fourth time he stood with his hand upon it, and then with sudden resolution flung it open and walked up the path. Mrs. White at the same moment placed her hands behind her, and hurriedly unfastening the strings of her apron, put that useful article of apparel beneath the cushion of her chair.

She brought the stranger, who seemed ill at ease, into the room. He gazed at her furtively, and listened in a preoccupied fashion as the old lady apologized for the appearance of the room, and her husband's coat, a garment which he usually reserved for the garden. She then waited, as patiently as she could, for him to broach his business, but he was at first strangely silent.

"I—was asked to call," he said at last, and stooped and picked up a piece of cotton from his trousers. "I come from 'Maw and Meggins'."

The old lady started. "Is anything the matter?" she asked breathlessly. "Has anything happened to Herbert? What is it? What is it?"

Her husband interposed. "There, there, mother," he said hastily. "Sit down, and don't jump to conclusions. You've not brought bad news, I'm sure, sir;" and he eyed the other wistfully.

"I'm sorry—" began the visitor.

"Is he hurt?" demanded the mother wildly.

The visitor bowed in assent. "Badly hurt," he said quietly, "but he is not in any pain."

"Oh, thank God!" said the old woman, clasping her hands. "Thank God for that! Thank—"

She broke off suddenly as the sinister meaning of the assurance dawned upon her and she saw the awful confirmation of her fears in the other's averted face. She caught her breath, and turning to her slower-witted husband, laid her trembling old hand upon his. There was a long silence.

"He was caught in the machinery," said the visitor at length in a low voice.

"Caught in the machinery," repeated Mr. White, in a dazed fashion, "yes."

He sat staring blankly out at the window, and taking his wife's hand between his own, pressed it as he had been wont to do in their old courting days nearly forty years before.

"He was the only one left to us," he said, turning gently to the visitor. "It is hard."

The other coughed, and rising, walked slowly to the window. "The firm wished me to convey their sincere sympathy with you in your great loss," he said, without looking round. "I beg that you will understand I am only their servant and merely obeying orders."

There was no reply; the old woman's face was white, her eyes staring, and her breath inaudible; on the husband's face was a look such as his friend the sergeant-major might have carried into his first action.

"I was to say that Maw and Meggins disclaim all responsibility," continued the other. "They admit no liability at all, but in consideration of your son's services, they wish to present you with a certain sum as compensation."

Mr. White dropped his wife's hand, and rising to his feet, gazed with a look of horror at his visitor. His dry lips shaped the words, "How much?"

"Two hundred pounds," was the answer.

Unconscious of his wife's shriek, the old man smiled faintly, put out his hand like a sightless man, and dropped, a senseless heap, to the floor.

In the huge new cemetery, some three kilometres distant, the old people buried their dead, and came back to a house steeped in shadow and silence. It was all over so quickly that at first they could hardly realize it, and remained in a state of expectation as though of something else to happen— something else which was to lighten this load, too heavy for old hearts to bear.

But the days passed, and expectation gave place to resignation—the hopeless resignation of the old, sometimes miscalled apathy. Sometimes they hardly exchanged a word, for now they had nothing to talk about, and their days were long to weariness.

It was about a week after that the old man, waking suddenly in the night, stretched out his hand and found himself alone. The room was in darkness, and the sound of subdued weeping came from the window. He raised himself in bed and listened.

"Come back," he said tenderly. "You will be cold."

"It is colder for my son," said the old woman, and wept afresh.

The sound of her sobs died away on his ears. The bed was warm and his eyes heavy with sleep. He dozed fitfully, and then slept until a sudden wild cry from his wife awoke him with a start.

"*The paw!*" she cried wildly. "The monkey's paw!"

He started up in alarm. "Where? Where is it? What's the matter?"

She came stumbling across the room towards him. "I want it," she said quietly. "You've not destroyed it?"

"It's in the parlour, on the bracket," he replied, marvelling. "Why?"

She cried and laughed together, and bending over, kissed his cheek.

"I only just thought of it," she said hysterically. "Why didn't I think of it before? Why didn't *you* think of it?"

"Think of what?" he questioned.

"The other two wishes," she replied rapidly. "We've only had one."

"Was not that enough?" he demanded fiercely.

"No," she cried triumphantly; "we'll have one more. Go down and get it quickly, and wish our boy alive again."

The man sat up in bed and flung the bedclothes from his quaking limbs. "Good God, are you mad!" he cried, aghast.

"Get it," she panted; "Get it quickly, and wish—Oh, my boy, my boy!"

Her husband struck a match and lit the candle. "Get back to bed," he said unsteadily. "You don't know what you are saying."

"We had the first wish granted," said the old woman feverishly; "why not the second?"

"A coincidence," stammered the old man.

"Go and get it and wish," cried his wife, quivering with excitement.

The old man turned and regarded her, and his voice shook. "He has been dead ten days, and besides he—I would not tell you else, but—I could only recognize him by his clothing. If he was too terrible for you to see then, how now?"

"Bring him back," cried the old woman, and dragged him towards the door. "Do you think I fear the child I have nursed?"

He went down in the darkness, and felt his way to the parlour, and then to the mantelpiece. The talisman was in its place, and a horrible fear that the unspoken wish might bring his mutilated son before him ere he could escape from the room seized upon him, and he caught his breath as he found that he had lost the direction of the door. His brow cold with sweat, he felt his way round the table, and groped along the wall until he found himself in the small passage with the unwholesome thing in his hand.

Even his wife's face seemed changed as he entered the room. It was white and expectant, and to his fears seemed to have an unnatural look upon it. He was afraid of her.

"*Wish!*" she cried, in a strong voice.

"It is foolish and wicked," he faltered.

"*Wish*!" repeated his wife.

He raised his hand. "I wish my son alive again."

The talisman fell to the floor, and he regarded it fearfully. Then he sank trembling into a chair as the old woman, with burning eyes, walked to the window and raised the blind.

He sat until he was chilled with the cold, glancing occasionally at the figure of the old woman peering through the window. The candle-end, which had burned below the rim of the china candlestick, was throwing pulsating shadows on the ceiling and walls, until, with a flicker larger than the rest, it expired. The old man, with an unspeakable sense of relief at the failure of the talisman, crept back to his bed, and a minute or two afterward the old woman came silently and apathetically beside him.

Neither spoke, but lay silently listening to the ticking of the clock. A stair creaked, and a squeaky mouse scurried noisily through the wall. The darkness was oppressive, and after lying for some time screwing up his courage, he took the box of matches, and striking one, went downstairs for a candle.

At the foot of the stairs the match went out, and he paused to strike another; and at the same moment a knock, so quiet and stealthy as to be scarcely audible, sounded on the front door.

The matches fell from his hand and spilled in the passage. He stood motionless, his breath suspended until the knock was repeated. Then he turned and fled swiftly back to his room, and closed the door behind him. A third knock sounded through the house.

"*What's that*?" cried the old woman, starting up.

"A rat," said the old man in shaking tones—"a rat. It passed me on the stairs."

His wife sat up in bed listening. A loud knock resounded through the house.

"It's Herbert!" she screamed. "It's Herbert!"

She ran to the door, but her husband was before her, and catching her by the arm, held her tightly.

"What are you doing?" he whispered hoarsely.

"It's my boy; it's Herbert!" she cried, struggling mechanically. "I forgot it was three kilometres away. What are you holding me for? Let go. I must open the door."

"For God's sake, don't let it in," cried the old man, trembling.

"You're afraid of your own son," she cried, struggling. "Let me go. I'm coming, Herbert; I'm coming."

There was another knock, and another. The old woman with a sudden wrench broke free and ran from the room. Her husband followed to the landing, and called after her appealingly as she hurried downstairs. He heard the chain rattle back and the bottom bolt drawn slowly and stiffly from the socket. Then the old woman's voice, strained and panting.

"The bolt," she cried loudly. "Come down. I can't reach it."

But her husband was on his hands and knees groping wildly on the floor in search of the paw. If he could only find it before the thing outside got in. A perfect fusillade of knocks reverberated through the house, and he heard the scraping of a chair as his wife put it down in the passage against the door. He heard the creaking of the bolt as it came slowly back, and the same moment he found the monkey's paw, and frantically breathed his third and last wish.

The knocking ceased suddenly, although the echoes of it were still in the house. He heard the chair drawn back, and the door opened. A cold wind rushed up the staircase, and a long loud wail of disappointment and misery from his wife gave him the courage to run down to her side, and then to the gate beyond. The street lamp flickering opposite shone on a quiet deserted road.

———

What would your second two wishes have been?

Why do you suppose this story has remained so popular over the years? (It was first published in 1902.)

If you were making a film of this story, how would you design the set? How would you cast the characters? What special effects would you use?

Nothing Happens on the Moon

BY PAUL ERNST

On the bottom of the pit a rock was moving. It was moving, not as if it had volition of its own, but as if it were being handled by some unseen thing. Finally it rose from the ground and hung poised about two metres in the air!

The shining ball of the full Earth floated like a smooth pearl between two vast, angular mountains. The full Earth. Another month had ticked by.

Clow Hartigan turned from the porthole beside the small air lock to the Bliss radio transmitter.

"RC3, RC3, RC3," he droned out.

There was no answer. Stacey, up in New York, always took his time about answering the RC3 signal, confound it! But then, why shouldn't he? There was never anything of importance to listen to from station RC3. Nothing of any significance ever happened on the moon.

Hartigan stared unseeingly at the pink cover of a six-month-old *Radio Gazette* pasted to the wall over the control board.

"RC3, RC3—"

Ah, there Stacey was, the pompous little busybody.

"Hartigan talking. Monthly report."

"Go ahead, Hartigan."

A hurried, fussy voice. Calls of real import waited for Stacey; calls from Venus and Jupiter and Mars. Hurry up, Moon, and report that nothing has happened, as usual.

Hartigan proceeded to do so.

"Lunar conditions the same. No ships have put in, or have reported themselves as being in distress. The hangar is in good shape, with no leaks. Nothing out of the way has occurred."

"Right," said Stacey pompously. "Supplies?"

"You might send up a replacement," said Hartigan.

"Be serious. Need anything?"

"No." Hartigan's eyes brooded. "How's everything in Little Old New York?"

Stacey's businesslike voice was a reproof. Also it was a pain in the neck.

"Sorry. Can't gossip. Things pretty busy around here. If you need anything, let me know."

The burr of power went dead. Hartigan cursed with monotony, and got up.

Clow Hartigan was a big man with sand-red hair and slightly bitter eyes. He was representative of the type Spaceways sent to such isolated emergency landing-stations as the Moon.

There were half a dozen such emergency landing-domes, visited only by supply ships, exporting nothing, but ready in case some passenger liner was crippled by a meteor or by mechanical trouble. The two worst on the Spaceways list were the insulated hell on Mercury, and this great, lonely hangar on the Moon. To them Spaceways sent the pick of their probation executives. Big men. Powerful men. Young men. Also men who were unlucky enough not to have an old family friend or an uncle on the board of directors who could swing a soft berth for them. Spaceways did not keep them there long. Men killed themselves, or went mad and began inconsiderately smashing expensive equipment, after too long a dose of such loneliness as that of the Moon.

Hartigan went back to the porthole beside the small air lock. As he went, he talked to himself, as men do when they have been too long away from their own kind.

"I wish I'd brought a dog up here, or a cat. I wish there'd be an attempted raid. Anything at all. If only something would happen."

Resentfully he stared out at the photographic, black and white lunar landscape, lighted coldly by the full Earth. From that his eye went to the deep black of the heavens. Then his heart gave a jump. There was a faint light up there where no light was supposed to be.

He hurried to the telescope and studied it. A space liner, and a big one. Out of its course, no matter where it was bound, or it couldn't have been seen from the Moon with the naked eye. Was it limping in here to the emergency landing for repairs?

"I don't wish them any bad luck," muttered Hartigan, "But I hope they've burned out a rocket tube."

Soon his heart sank, however. The liner soared over the landing dome a hundred and sixty kilometres up, and went serenely on its way. In a short time its light faded in the distance. Probably it was one of the luxurious round-the-solar-system ships, passing close to the Moon to give the sightseers an intimate glimpse of it, but not stopping because there was absolutely nothing of interest here.

"Nothing ever happens on this forsaken rock," Hartigan gritted.

Impatiently he took his space suit down from the rack. Impatiently he stepped into the bulky, flexible metal thing and clamped down the head-piece. Nothing else to do. He'd take a walk. The red beam of the radio control board would summon him back to the hangar if for any reason anyone tried to raise RC3.

He let himself out through the double wall of the small air lock and set out with easy, four-metre strides toward a nearby cliff on the brink of which it was sometimes his habit to sit and think nasty thoughts of people who ran Spaceways and maintained places like RC3.

Between the hangar and the cliff was a wide expanse of grey lava ash, a sort of small lake of the stuff, feathery fine. Hartigan did not know how deep it might be. He did know that a man could probably sink down in it so far that he would never be able to burrow out again.

He turned to skirt the lake of lava ash, but paused a moment before proceeding.

Behind him loomed the enormous half-globe of the hangar, like a phosphorescent mushroom in the blackness. One section of the half-globe was flattened; and here were the gigantic inner and outer portals where a liner's rocket-propelled life shells could enter the dome. The great doors of this, the main air lock, reared halfway to the top of the hangar, and weighed several hundred tonnes apiece.

Before him was the face of the Moon: sharp angles of rock; jagged tremendous mountains; sheer, deep craters; all picked out in black and white from the reflected light of Earth.

A desolate prospect. . .Hartigan started on.

The ash beside him suddenly seemed to explode, soundlessly but with great violence. It spouted up like a geyser to a distance of thirty metres, hung for an instant over him in a spreading cloud, then quickly began to settle.

A meteor! Must have been a fair-sized one to have made such a splash in the volcanic dust.

"Close call," muttered Hartigan, voice sepulchral in his helmet. "A little nearer and they'd be sending a new man to the lunar emergency dome."

But he only grinned and went on. Meteors were like lightning back on Earth. Either they hit you or they missed. There was no warning till after they struck; then it was too late to do anything about it.

Hartigan stumbled over something in the cloud of ash that was sifting down around him. Looking down, he saw a smooth, round object, black-hot, about as big as his head.

"The meteor," he observed, "must have hit a slanting surface at the bottom of the ash heap and ricocheted up and out here. I wonder—"

He stooped clumsily toward it. His right "hand," which was a heavy pincer arrangement terminating the right sleeve of his suit, went out, then his left, and with some difficulty he picked the thing up. Now and then a meteor held splashes of precious metals. Sometimes one was picked up that yielded several hundred dollars' worth of platinum or iridium. A little occasional gravy with which the emergency-landing exiles could buy amusement when they got back home.

Through the annoying shower of ash he could see dimly the light of the hangar. He started back, to get out of his suit and analyze the meteor for possible value.

It was the oddest-looking thing he had ever seen come out of the heavens. In the first place, its shape was remarkable. It was perfectly round, instead of being irregular as were most meteors.

"Like an old-fashioned cannon ball," Hartigan mused, bending over it on a workbench. "Or an egg—"

Eyebrows raised whimsically, he played with the idea.

"Jupiter! What an egg it would be! Fifty-four kilograms if it's a gram, and it smacked the Moon like a bullet without even cracking! I wouldn't want it poached for breakfast."

The next thing to catch his attention was the projectile's odd colour, or rather, odd way in which the colour seemed to be changing. It had been dull, black-hot, when Hartigan brought it in. It was now a dark green, and was getting lighter swiftly as it cooled!

The big clock struck a mellow note. Time for the dome keeper to make his daily inspection of the main doors.

Reluctantly Hartigan left the odd meteor, which was now as green as grass and actually seemed to be growing transparent, and walked toward the big air lock.

He switched on the radio power unit. There was no power plant of any kind in the hangar; all power was broadcast by the Spaceways central station. He reached for the contact switch which poured the invisible Niagara of power into the motors that moved the ponderous doors.

Cr-r-rack!

Like a cannon shot the sound split the air in the huge metal dome, echoing from wall to wall, to die at last in a muffled rumbling.

White-faced, Hartigan was running long before the echoes died away. He ran toward the workbench he had recently quitted. The sound seemed to have come from near there. His thought was that the hangar had been crashed by a meteor larger than its cunningly braced beams, tough metal sheath, and artful angles of deflection would stand.

That would mean death, for the air supply in the dome would race out through a fissure almost before he could don his space suit.

However, his anxious eyes, scanning the vaulting roof, could find no crumpled bracing or ominous downward bulges. And he could hear no thin whine of air surging in the hangar to the almost non-existent pressure outside.

Then he glanced at the workbench, and uttered an exclamation. The meteor he had left there was gone.

"It must have rolled off the bench," he told himself. "But if it's on the floor, why can't I see it?"

He froze into movelessness. Had that been a sound behind him? A sound, where no sound could possibly be made save by himself?

He whirled—and saw nothing. Nothing whatever, save the familiar expanse of smooth rock floor lighted with the cold white illumination broadcast on the power band.

He turned back to the workbench where the meteor had been, and began feeling over it with his hands, disbelieving the evidence of his eyes.

Another exclamation burst from his lips as his finger touched something hard and smooth and round. The meteor. Broken into two halves, but still there. Only now it was invisible!

"This," said Hartigan, beginning to sweat a little, "is the craziest thing I ever heard of!"

He picked up one of the two invisible halves and held it close before his eyes. He could not see it at all, though it was solid to the touch. Moreover, he seemed able to see through it, for nothing on the other side was blotted out.

Fear increased within him as his fingers told him that the two halves were empty, hollow. Heavy as the ball had been, it consisted of nothing but a shell about five centimetres thick. Unless—

"Unless something really did crawl out of it when it split apart."

But that, of course, was ridiculous.

"It's just an ordinary metallic chunk," he told himself, "that split open with a loud bang when it cooled, due to contraction. The only thing unusual about it is its invisibility. That is strange."

He groped on the workbench for the other half of the thick round shell. With a half in each hand, he started toward the stockroom, meaning to lock up this odd substance very carefully. He suspected he had something beyond price here. If he could go back to Earth with a substance that could produce invisibility, he could become one of the richest men in the universe.

He presented a curious picture as he walked over the brilliantly lighted floor. His shoulders sloped down with the weight of the two pieces of meteor. His bare arms rippled and knotted with muscular effort. Yet his hands seemed empty. So far as the eye could tell, he was carrying nothing whatever.

"What—"

He dropped the halves of the shell with a ringing clang, and began leaping toward the big doors. That time he knew he had heard a sound, a sound like scurrying steps! It had come from near the big doors.

When he got there, however, he could hear nothing. For a time the normal stillness, the ghastly, phenomenal stillness, was preserved. Then from near the spot he had just vacated, he heard another noise. This time it was a gulping, voracious noise, accompanied by a sound that was like that of a rock crusher or concrete mixer in action.

On the run, he returned, seeing nothing all this while but smooth rock floor and plain, metal-ribbed walls, and occasional racks of instruments.

He got to the spot where he had dropped the parts of the meteor. The parts were no longer there. This time it was more than a question of invisibility. They had disappeared actually as well as visually.

To make sure, Hartigan got down on his knees and searched every centimetre of a large circle. There was no trace of the thick shell.

"Either something brand-new to the known solar system is going on here," Hartigan declared, "or I'm getting as crazy as they insisted poor Stuyvesant was."

Increased perspiration glinted on his forehead. The fear of madness in the lonelier emergency fields was a very real fear. United Spaceways had been petitioned more than once to send two men instead of one to manage each outlying field; but Spaceways was an efficient corporation with no desire to pay two men where one could handle the job.

Again Hartigan could hear nothing at all. And in swift though unadmitted fear that perhaps the whole business had transpired only in his own brain, he sought refuge in routine. He returned to his task of testing the big doors, which was important even though dreary in its daily repetition.

The radio power unit was on, as he left it. He closed the circuit.

Smoothly the enormous inner doors swung open on their broad tracks, to reveal the equally enormous outer portals. Hartigan stepped into the big air lock, and closed the inner doors. He shivered a little. It was near freezing out here in spite of the heating units.

There was a small control room in the lock, to save an operator the trouble of getting into a space suit when the doors were opened. Hartigan entered this and pushed home the switch that moved the outer portals.

Smoothly, perfectly, their tremendous bulk opened outward. They always worked smoothly, perfectly. No doubt they always would. Nevertheless, rules said test them regularly. And it was best to live up to the rules. With characteristic trustfulness, Spaceways had recording dials in the home station that showed by power markings whether or not their planetary employees were doing what they were supposed to do.

Hartigan reversed the switch. The doors began to close. They got to the halfway mark; to the three-quarters—

Hartigan felt rather than heard the sharp, grinding jar. He felt rather than heard the high, shrill scream, a rasping shriek, almost above the limit of audibility, that was something to make a man's blood run cold.

Still, without faltering, the doors moved inward and their serrated edges met. Whatever one of them had ground across had not been large enough to shake it.

"Jupiter!" Hartigan breathed, once more inside the huge dome with both doors closed.

He sat down to try to think the thing out.

"A smooth, round meteor falls. It looks like an egg, though it seems to be of metallic rock. As it cools, it gets lighter in colour, till finally it disappears. With a loud bang, it bursts apart, and afterward I hear a sound like scurrying feet. I drop the pieces of the shell to go toward the sound, and then I hear another sound, as if something were macerating and gulping down pieces of shell, eating them. I come back and can't find the pieces. I go on with my test of opening and closing the main doors. As the outer door closes, I hear a crunching noise as if a rock were being pulverized, and a high scream like that of an animal in pain. All this would indicate that the meteor was a shell, and that some living thing did come out of it.

"But that is impossible.

"No form of life could live through a crash with which that thing struck the Moon, even though the lava ash did cushion the fall to some extent. No form of life could stand the heat of the meteor's fall and impact. No form of life could eat the rocky, metallic shell. It's utterly impossible.

"Or—is it impossible?"

He gnawed at his knuckles and thought of Stuyvesant. Stuyvesant had been assigned to the emergency dome on Mercury. There was a place for you! An inferno! By miracles of insulation and supercooling systems the hangar there had been made livable. But the finest of space suits could not keep a man from frying to death outside. Nothing to do except stay cooped up inside the hangar, and pray for the six-month relief to come.

Stuyvesant had done that. And from Stuyvesant had begun to come queer reports. He thought he had seen something moving on Mercury near his landing-field. Something like a rock!

Moving rocks. With the third report of that kind, the corporation had brought him home and turned him over to the board of science for examination. Poor Stuyvesant had barely escaped the lunatic asylum. He had been let out of Spaceways, of course. The corporation scrapped men suspected of being defective as quickly as they scrapped suspect material.

"When a man begins to see rocks moving, it's time to fire him," was the unofficial verdict.

The board of science had coldly said the same thing, though in more dignified language.

"No form of life as we know it could possibly exist in the high temperature and desert conditions of Mercury. Therefore, in our judgment, Benjamin Stuyvesant suffered from hallucination when he reported some rocklike entity moving near Emergency Hangar RC10."

Hartigan glanced uneasily toward the workbench on which the old meteor had rested.

"No form of life as we know it."

There was the catch. After all, this interplanetary travel was less than seventy years old. Might there not be many things still unknown to Earth wisdom?

"Not to hear the board of science tell it," muttered Hartigan, thinking of Stuyvesant's blasted career.

He thought of the Forbidden Asteroids. There were over two dozen on the charts on which, even in direst emergency, no ship was supposed to land. That was because ships had landed there, and had vanished without trace. Again and again. With no one able to dream of their fate. Till they simply marked the little globes "Forbidden," and henceforth ignored them.

"No form of life as we know it!"

Suppose something savage, huge, invisible, lived on those grim asteroids? Something that developed from egg form? Something that spread its young through the universe by propelling eggs from one celestial body to another? Something that started growth by devouring its own metallic shell, and continued it on a mineral instead of vegetable diet? Something that could live in any atmosphere or temperature?

"I am going crazy," Hartigan breathed.

In something like panic he tried to forget the affair in a great stack of books and magazines brought by the last supply ship.

The slow hours of another month ticked by. The full Earth waned, died, grew again. Drearily Hartigan went through the monotony of his routine. Day after day, the term "day" being a strictly figurative one on this drear lunar lump.

He rose at six, New York Time, and sponged off carefully in a bit of precious water. He ate breakfast. He read. He stretched his muscles in a stroll. He read. He inspected his equipment. He read. He exercised on a set of homemade flying rings. He read.

"No human being should be called on to live like this," he said once, his voice too loud and brittle.

But human beings did have to live like this, if they aspired to one of the big posts on a main planet.

He had almost forgotten the strange meteor that had fallen into lava ash at his feet a month ago. It was to be recalled with terrible abruptness.

He went for a walk in a direction he did not usually take, and came upon a shallow pit a kilometre from the dome. Pits, of course, are myriad on the Moon. The whole surface is made up of craters within craters. But this pit was not typical in conformation. Most are smooth-walled and flat-bottomed. This pit was ragged, as if it had been dug out. Besides, Hartigan had thought he knew every hole around the hangar, and he did not remember ever seeing this one.

He stood on its edge looking down. There was loose rock in its uncrater-like bottom, and the loose rock had the appearance of being freshly dislodged. Even this was not unusual in a place where the vibration of a footstep could sometimes cause tonnes to crack and fall.

Nevertheless, Hartigan could feel the hair rise a bit on the back of his neck as some deep, instinctive fear crawled within him at the sight of the small, shallow pit. And then he caught his lips between his teeth and stared with wide, unbelieving eyes.

On the bottom of the pit a rock was moving. It was moving, not as if it had volition of its own, but as if it were being handled by some unseen thing.

A fragment about as big as his body, it rolled over twice, then slid along in impatient jerks as though a big head or hoof nudged at it. Finally it rose from the ground and hung poised about two metres in the air!

Breathlessly, Hartigan watched, while all his former, almost superstitious, fear flooded through him.

The rock fragment moved up and down in mid-space.

"Jupiter!" Clow Hartigan breathed hoarsely.

A large part of one end suddenly disappeared. A pointed projection from the main mass of rock, it broke off and vanished from sight.

Another large chunk followed, breaking off and disappearing as though by magic.

"Jupiter!"

There was no longer doubt in Hartigan's mind. A live thing had emerged from the egglike meteor twenty-seven days ago. A live thing, that now roamed loose over the face of the Moon.

But that section of rock, which was apparently being devoured, was held two metres off the ground. What manner of creature could come from an egg no larger than his head and grow in one short month into a thing over two metres tall? He thought of the Forbidden Asteroids, where no ships landed, though no man knew precisely what threat lurked there.

"It must be as big as a mastodon," Hartigan whispered. "What in the universe—?"

The rock fragment was suddenly dropped, as if whatever invisible thing had held it had suddenly seen Hartigan at the rim of the pit. Then the rock was dashed to one side as if by a charging body. The next instant loose fragments of shale scattered right and left up one side of the pit as though a big body were climbing up and out.

The commotion in the shale was on the side of the pit nearest Hartigan. With a cry he ran toward the hangar.

With fantastic speed, eighteen and twenty metres to a jump, he covered the ragged surface. But fast as he moved, he felt that the thing behind him moved faster. And that there was something behind him he did not doubt for an instant, though he could neither see nor hear it.

It was weird, this pygmy human form in its bulky space suit flying soundlessly over the lunar surface under the glowing ball of Earth, racing like mad for apparently no reason at all, running insanely when, so far as the eye could tell, nothing pursued.

But abysmal instinct told Hartigan that he was pursued, all right. And instinct told him that he could never reach the hangar in the lead. With desperate calmness he searched the ground still lying between him and the hangar.

A little ahead was a crack about thirty metres wide and, as far as he knew, bottomless. With his oversized Earth muscles he could clear that in a gigantic leap. Could the ponderous, invisible thing behind him leap that far?

He was in mid-flight long enough to turn his head and look back, as he hurtled the chasm in a prodigious jump. He saw a flurry among the rocks at the edge he had just left as something jumped after him. Then he came down on the far side, lighting in full stride like a hurdler.

He risked slowing his speed by looking back again. A second time he saw a flurry of loose rock, this time on the near side of the deep crack. The thing had not quite cleared the edge, it seemed.

He raced on and came to a small air-lock door. He flung himself inside. He had hardly got the fastener in its groove when something banged against the outside of the door.

The thing pursuing him had hung on the chasm's edge long enough to let him reach safety, but had not fallen into the black depths as he had hoped it might.

"But that's all right," he said, drawing a great sigh of relief as he entered the hangar through the inner door. "I don't care what it does, now that I'm inside and it's out."

He got out of the space suit, planning as he moved. The thing outside was over two metres tall and made of some unflesh-like substance that must be practically indestructible. At its present rate of growth it would be as big as a small space liner in six months, if it weren't destroyed. But it would have to be destroyed. Either that, or Emergency Station RC3 would have to be abandoned, and his job with it, which concerned him more than the station.

"I'll call Stacey to send a destroyer," he said crisply.

He moved toward the Bliss transmitter, eyes glinting.

Things were happening on the Moon, now, all right! And the thing that was happening was going to prove Stuyvesant as sane as any man, much saner than the grey-bearded goats on the board of science.

He would be confined to the hangar till Stacey could send a destroyer. No more strolls. He shuddered a little as he thought of how many times he must have barely missed death in his walks during the past month.

Hartigan got halfway to the Bliss transmitter, skirting along the wall near the small air lock.

A dull, hollow, booming sound filled the great hangar, ascending to the vaulted roof and seeming to shower down again like black water.

Hartigan stopped and stared at the wall beside him. It was bulging inward a little. Startled out of all movement, he stared at the ominous, slight bulge. And as he stared, the booming noise repeated, and the bulge grew a bit larger.

"In the name of Heaven!"

The thing outside had managed to track him along the wall from the air lock, perhaps guided by the slight vibration of his steps. Now it was blindly charging the huge bulk of the hangar like a living, ferocious ram.

A third time the dull, terrible booming sound reverberated in the lofty hangar. The bulge in the tough metal gave ever so little at the points of strain. Hartigan moved back toward the air lock. While he moved, there was silence. The moment he stopped, there was another dull, booming crash and a second bulge appeared in the wall. The thing had followed him precisely, and was trying to get at him.

The colour drained from Hartigan's face. This changed the entire scheme of things.

It was useless to radio for help now. Long before a destroyer could get here, the savage, insensate monster outside would have opened a rent in the wall. That would mean Hartigan's death from escaping air in the hangar.

Crash!

Who would have dreamed that there lived anywhere in the universe on no matter how far or wild a globe, a creature actually able to damage the massive walls of a Spaceways hangar? He could see himself trying to tell about this.

"An animal big enought to crack a hangar wall? And invisible? Well!"

Crash!

The very light globes, so far overhead, seemed to quiver a bit with the impact of this thing of unguessable nature against the vast semisphere of the hangar. The second bulge was deep enough so that the white enamel which coated it began chipping off in little flakes at the bulge's apex.

"What the devil am I going to do?"

The only thing he could think of for the moment was to move along the wall. That unleashed giant outside must not concentrate too long on any one spot.

He walked a dozen steps. As before, the ramming stopped while he was in motion, to start again as he halted. As before, it started at the point nearest to him.

Once more a bulge appeared in the wall, this time bigger that either of the first two. The metal sheets sheathing the hangar varied a little in strength. The invisible terror outside had struck a soft spot.

Hartigan hastily moved to another place.

"The whole base of the hangar will be scalloped like a pie crust at this rate," he gritted. "What can I—"

Crash!

He had inadvertently stopped near a rack filled with spare power bulbs. With its ensuing attack the blind fury had knocked the rack down on the floor.

Hartigan's jaw set hard. Whatever he did must be done quickly. And it must be done by himself alone. He could not stay at the Bliss transmitter long enough to get New York and tell what was wrong, without giving the gigantic thing outside a fatal number of minutes in which to concentrate on one section of wall.

He moved slowly around the hangar, striving to keep the invisible fury too occupied in following him to get in more than an occasional charge. As he walked, his eyes went from one heap of supplies to another in search of a possible means of defence.

There were ordinary weapons in plenty, in racks along the wall, but none of these, he knew, could do material harm to the attacking fury.

He got to the great inner doors of the main air lock in his slow march round the hangar. And here he stopped, eyes glowing thoughtfully.

The huge doors had threatened in the early days to be the weak points in the Spaceways hangars. So the designers, like good engineers, had made the doors so massive that in the end they were stronger than the walls round them.

Bang!

A bulge near the massive hinges told Hartigan that the thing outside was as relentless as ever in its effort to break through the wall and get at him. But he paid no attention to the new bulge. He was occupied with the doors.

If the invisible giant could be trapped in the main air lock between the outer and inner portals—

"Then what?" Hartigan wondered.

He could not answer his own question. But, anyway, it seemed like a step in the right direction to have the attacking fury penned between the doors rather than to have it loose and able to charge the more vulnerable walls.

"If I can coop it in the air lock, I might be able to think of some way to attack it," he went on.

He pushed home the control switch which set the broadcast power to opening the outer doors. And that gave him an idea that sent a wild thrill surging through him.

A heavy rumble told him the motors were swinging open the outer doors.

"Will the thing come in?" he asked himself tensely. "Or has it sense enough to scent a trap?"

Bang!

The inner doors trembled a little on their broad tracks. The invisible monster had entered the trap.

"Trap?" Hartigan smiled mirthlessly. "Not much of a trap. Left to itself, it could probably break out in half an hour. But it won't be left to itself."

He reversed the switch to close the outer portals. Then, with the doors closed and the monster penned between, he got to work on the idea that had been born when he pushed the control switch.

Power, oceans of it, flooded from the power unit at the touch of a finger. A docile servant when properly channelled, it could be the deadliest thing on the Moon.

He ran back down the hangar to the stockroom, and got out a drum of spare power cable. As quickly as was humanly possible, he rolled the drum back to the doors, unwinding the cable as he went.

It was with grim solemnity that he made his next move. He had to open the inner doors a few centimetres to go on with his frail plan of defence. And he had to complete the plan before the thing in the air lock could claw them open still more and charge through. For all their weight the doors rolled in perfect balance; and if the unseen terror could make dents in the solid wall, it certainly was strong enough to move the partly opened doors.

Speed! That was the thing that would make or break him. Speed, and hope that the power unit could stand a terrific overload without blowing a tube.

With a hand that inclined to tremble a bit, Hartigan moved the control switch operating the inner doors, and instantly cut the circuit again.

The doors opened fifteen centimetres or so, and stopped.

Hartigan cut off the power unit entirely, and dragged the end of the spare power cable to it. With flying fingers he disconnected the cable leading from the control switch to the motors that moved the portals, and connected the spare cable in its place.

He glanced anxiously at the doors, and saw that the opening between them had more than doubled. The left door moved a little even as he watched.

"I'll never make it!"

But he went ahead.

Grabbing up the loose end of the cable, he threw it in a tangled coil as far as he could through the opening and into the air lock. Then he leaped for the power unit—and watched.

The cable lay unmoving on the air-lock floor. But the left door moved! It jerked, and rolled open another fifteen centimetres.

Hartigan clenched his hands as he stared at the inert cable. He had counted on the blind ferocity of the invisible terror; had counted on its attacking, or at least touching, the cable immediately. Had it enough intelligence to realize dimly that it would be best to avoid the cable? Was it going to keep on working at those doors till—

The power cable straightened with a jerk. Straightened and hung still, with a loose end suspended in mid-air almost two metres off the air-lock floor.

Hartigan's hand slammed down. The broadcast power was turned to the last notch.

With his heart hammering in his throat, Hartigan gazed through the opening between the doors. Gazed at the cable through which was coursing oceans, Niagaras, of power. And out there in the air lock a thing began to build up from thin air into a spectacle that made him cry out in wild horror.

He got a glimpse of a massive block of a head, eyeless and featureless, that joined with no neck whatever to a barrel of a body. He got a glimpse of five legs, like stone pillars, and of a sixth that was a stump. ("That's what got caught in the doors a month ago—its leg," he heard himself babbling with insane calmness.) Over three metres high and six metres long, the thing was a living battering-ram, painted in the air in sputtering, shimmering blue sparks that streamed from its huge bulk in all directions.

Just a glimpse he got, and then the monster began to scream as it had the first day when the door maimed it. Only now it was with a volume that tore at Hartigan's eardrums till he screamed himself in agony.

As he watched, he saw the huge carcass melt a little, like wax in flame, with the power cable also melting slowly and fusing into the cavernous, rocky jaws that had seized it. Then with a rush the whole bulk disintegrated into a heap of loose mineral matter.

Hartigan turned off the power unit and collapsed, with his face in his hands.

The shining ball of the full Earth floated like a smooth diamond between two vast, angular mountains. The full Earth.

Hartigan turned from the porthole beside the small air lock and strode to the Bliss radio transmitter. "RC3, RC3, RC3," he droned out.

There was no answer. As usual, Stacey was taking his time answering the Moon's signal.

"RC3, RC3—"

There he was.

"Hartigan talking. Monthly report."

"All right, Hartigan."

A hurried, fretful voice. Come on, Moon; report that as always, nothing has happened.

"Lunar conditions the same," said Hartigan. "No ships have put in, or have reported themselves as being in distress. The hangar is in good shape, with no leaks."

"Right," said Stacey, in the voice of a busy man. "Supplies?"

"You might send up a replacement."

"Be serious, please. Supplies?"

"I need some new power bulbs."

"I'll send them on the next ship. Nothing irregular to report?"

Hartigan hesitated.

On the floor of the main air lock was a mound of burned, bluish mineral substance giving no indication whatever that it had once possessed outlandish, incredible life. In the walls of the hangar at the base were a half a dozen new dents; but ricocheting meteors might have made those. The meteoric shell from which this bizarre animal had come had been devoured, so even that was not left for investigation.

He remembered the report of the board of science on Stuyvesant.

"Therefore, in our judgment, Benjamin Stuyvesant suffered from hallucination—"

He would have liked to help Stuyvesant. But on the other hand Stuyvesant had a job with a second-hand space-suit store now, and was getting along pretty well in spite of Spaceways' dismissal.

"Nothing irregular to report?" repeated Stacey.

Hartigan stared, with one eyebrow sardonically raised, at the plump brunette on the pink Radio Gazette cover pasted to the wall.

"Nothing irregular to report," Hartigan said steadily.

———

How does Paul Ernst first signal that something **will** happen on the moon?

Should Hartigan have kept silent? Would you have?

The Old Man

BY HOLLOWAY HORN

From the darkness a paper was thrust at Knocker, whose unwilling fingers closed on it. A laugh came from somewhere in the recesses in the passage, and Knocker was alone.

Martin Thompson was not a desirable character. He possessed a clever, plausible tongue, and for years past had lived, with no little success, on his wits. He had promoted doubtful boxing competitions and still more doubtful sweepstakes. He had been a professional backer, in which capacity he had defrauded the bookies; again, a bookmaker who had swindled his "clients." There was more cunning than imagination in his outlook, but, within his limits, he possessed a certain distorted ability.

He was known to his intimates as Knocker Thompson, and as such had a surprisingly wide reputation. In outward appearance he was a gentleman, for long experience had taught him to avoid the flashy and distinctive in dress. Indeed, his quiet taste had often proved a valuable business asset.

Naturally, his fortunes varied, but he was usually more or less in funds. As Knocker sometimes said in his more genial moments: "For every mug that dies there's ten others born."

Funds were rather low, however, on the evening when he met the old man. Knocker had spent the early part of the evening with two acquaintances in a hotel near Leichester Square. It was a business meeting, and relations had been a little strained; opinions had been freely expressed which indicated a complete lack of confidence in Knocker, and an unmis-takable atmosphere had resulted. Not that he *resented* the opinions in the least, but at that juncture he *needed* the unquestioned trust of the two men.

He was not in the best of humours, therefore, as he turned into Whitcomb Street on his way to Charing Cross. The normal plainness of his features was deepened by a scowl, and the general result startled the few people who glanced at him.

But at eight o'clock in the evening, Whitcomb Street is not a crowded thoroughfare, and there was no one near them when the old man spoke to him. He was standing in a passage near the Pall Mall end, and Knocker could not see him clearly.

"Hullo, Knocker!" he said. Thompson swung around.

In the darkness he made out the dim figure, the most conspicuous feature of which was a long, white beard.

"Hullo!" returned Thompson, suspiciously, for as far as he knew he did not number among his acquaintances an old man with a white beard.

"It's cold. . ." said the old man.

"What d'you want?" asked Thompson curtly. "Who are you?"

"I am an old man, Knocker."

"Look here, what's the game? I don't know you. . ."

"No. But I know you."

"If that's all you've got to say. . ." said Knocker uneasily.

"It is nearly all. Will you buy a paper? It is not an ordinary paper, I assure you."

"How do you mean. . .not an ordinary paper?"

"It is tomorrow night's *Echo*," said the old man calmly.

"You're loopy, old chap, that's what's wrong with you. Look here, things aren't too brisk, but here's half a crown. . .and better luck!" For all his lack of principle, Knocker had the crude generosity of those who live precariously.

"Luck!" The old man laughed with a quietness that jarred on Knocker's nerves. In some queer way it seemed to run up and down his spine.

"Look here!" he said again, conscious of some strange, unreal quality in the old, dimly-seen figure in the passage. "What's the blinking game?"

"It is the oldest game in the world, Knocker."

"Not so free with my name...if you don't mind."

"Are you ashamed of it?"

"No," said Knocker stoutly. "What do you want? I've got no time to waste with the likes of you."

"Then go...Knocker."

"What do you *want*?" Knocker insisted, strangely uneasy.

"Nothing. Won't you take the paper? There is no other like it in the world. Nor will there be—for twenty-four hours."

"I don't suppose there *are* many of tomorrow's papers on sale... yet," said Knocker with a grin.

"It contains tomorrow's winners," said the old man, in the same casual manner.

"I don't think!" retorted Knocker.

"There it is; you may read for yourself."

From the darkness a paper was thrust at Knocker, whose unwilling fingers closed on it. A laugh came from somewhere in the recesses in the passage, and Knocker was alone.

He was suddenly and uncomfortably aware of his beating heart, but gripped himself and walked on until he came to a lighted shop front where he glanced at the paper.

"Thursday, July 29, 1926..." he read.

He thought a moment.

It was Wednesday...he was positive it was Wednesday. He took out his diary. It was Wednesday, the twenty-eighth day of July—the last day of the Kempton Park races. He had no doubt on the point, none whatever.

With a strange feeling he glanced at the paper again. July 29, 1926. He turned to the back page almost instinctively—the page with the racing results.

Gatwick...

That day's races were at Kempton Park. Tomorrow was the first day of the Gatwick races, and there, staring at him, were the five winners. He passed his hand across his forehead; it was damp with cold perspiration.

"There's a trick somewhere," he muttered to himself, and carefully re-examined the date of the paper. It was printed on each page...clear and unaltered. He scrutinized the unit figure of the year, but the "6" had not been tampered with.

He glanced hurriedly at the front page. There was a flaring headline about the Coal Strike...that wasn't twenty-*five*. With professional care he examined the racing results. Inkerman had won the first...Inkerman—and Knocker had made up his mind to back Paper Clip with more money than he could afford to lose. Paper Clip was merely an also-ran. He noticed that people who passed were glancing at him curiously. Hurriedly he pushed the paper into an inner pocket and walked on.

Never had Knocker so needed a drink. He entered a snug little "pub" near Charing Cross and was thankful to find the saloon bar nearly deserted. Fortified with his drink he turned again to the paper. Inkerman had come home at 6 to 1. He made certain hurried but satisfactory calculations. Salmon House had won the second; he had expected that, but not at such a price...7 to 4 on. Shallot—Shallot of all horses!—had romped away with the third, the big race. Seven lengths...at 100 to 8! Knocker licked his dry lips. There was no fake about the paper in his hand. He knew the horses that were running at Gatwick the following day and the results were there before him. The fourth and fifth winners were at short prices; but Inkerman and Shallot were enough...

It was too late to get in touch with any of the bookmakers that evening, and in any case it would not be advisable to put money on before the day of the race. The better way would be to go to Gatwick in the morning and wire the bets from the course.

He had another drink...and another.

Gradually, in the genial atmosphere of the saloon bar, his uneasiness left him. The affair ceased to appear uncanny and grotesque, and became a part of the casual happenings of the day. Into Knocker's slightly fuddled brain came the memory of a film he had once seen which had made a big impression on him at the time. There was an Eastern magician in the film, with a white beard, a long, white beard just like the one belonging to the old man. The magician had done the most extraordinary things...on the screen.

But whatever the explanation, Knocker was satisfied it was not a fake. The old chap had not asked for any money; indeed he had not even taken the half-crown that Knocker had offered him. And as Knocker knew, you always collected the dibs—or attempted to—if you were running a fake.

He thought pleasantly of what he would do in the ring at Gatwick the following day. He was in rather low water, but he could put his hands on just about enough to make the bookies sit up. And with a second winner at 100 to 8!

He had still another drink and stood the barman one too.

"D'you know anything for tomorrow?" The man behind the bar knew Thompson quite well by sight and reputation.

Knocker hesitated.

"Yes," he said. "Sure thing. Salmon House in the second race. Price'll be a bit short, but it's a snip."

"Thanks very much; I'll have a bit on meself."

Ultimately he left the saloon bar. He was a little shaky; his doctor had warned him not to drink, but surely on such a night. . .

The following morning he went to Gatwick. It was a meeting he liked, and usually he was very lucky there. But that day it was not merely a question of luck. There was a streak of caution in his bets on the first race, but he flung caution to the wind after Inkerman had come in a comfortable winner—*and at* 6 *to* 1. The horse and the price! He had no doubts left. Salmon House won the second, a hot favourite at 7 to 4 on.

In the big race most of the punters left Shallot alone. The horse had little form, and there was no racing reason why anyone should back him. He was among what the bookies call "the Rags." But Knocker cared nothing for "form" that day. He spread his money judiciously. Twenty here, twenty there. Not until ten minutes before the race did he wire any money to the West End offices, but some of the biggest men in the game opened their eyes when his wires came through. He was out to win a fortune. And he won.

As the horses entered the straight, one of them was lengths ahead of the field. It carried the flashing yellow and blue of Shallot's owner. The groan that went up from the punters around him was satisfactory, but there was no thrill in the race for him; he had been certain that Shallot would win. There was no objection. . .and he proceeded to collect.

His pockets were bulging with notes, but his winnings were as nothing compared with the harvest he would reap from the big men in the West End. He ordered a bottle of champagne, and with a silent grin drank the health of the old man with the beard before he sent for the taxi that would take him back to the station. There was no train for half an hour, and, when at last it started, his carriage was filled with racing men, among whom were several he knew.

Knocker was usually very expansive after a good day, but that afternoon he took no part in the conversation, with the exception of an occasional grunt when a remark was made to him. Try as he would he could not keep his thoughts away from the old man. It was the memory of the laugh that remained with him most vividly. He could still feel that queer sensation down his spine...

On a sudden impulse he took out the paper, which was still in his pocket. He had no real interest in news, as such, for racing absorbed the whole of his very limited imagination. As far as he could tell from a casual inspection is was a very ordinary sort of paper. He made up his mind to get another in town and compare the two in order to see if the old man had spoken the truth. Not that it mattered very much, he assured himself.

Suddenly, his incurious glance was held. A paragraph in the stop-press column had caught his eye. An exclamation burst from him.

"DEATH IN RACE-TRAIN," the paragraph was headed. Knocker's heart was pumping, but he read mechanically: Mr. Martin Thompson, a well-known racing man, died this afternoon as he was returning from Gatwick."

He got no further; the paper fell from his limp fingers onto the floor of the carriage.

"Look at Knocker," someone said. "He's ill..."

He was breathing heavily and with difficulty.

"Stop...stop the train," he gasped, and strove to rise and lurch towards the emergency cord.

"Steady on, Knocker," one of them said, and grasped his arm. "You sit down, old chap...musn't pull that darned thing...

He sat down...or rather collapsed into the seat. His head fell forward.

They forced whiskey between his lips, but it was of no avail.

"He's dead," came the awestruck voice of the man who held him.

No one noticed the paper on the floor. In the general upset it had been kicked under the seat, and it is not possible to say what became of it. Perhaps it was swept up by the cleaners at Waterloo.

Perhaps...

No one knows.

———

What did the author, Holloway Horn, want you to feel about Knocker? How do you know?

Would you want to know the future a day in advance? What would be the advantages? The disadvantages?

Hobbyist

BY FREDERIC BROWN

The druggist nodded. "Now," he said. "Tell me. Whom do you want to kill, and why?"

"I heard a rumour," Sangstrom said, "to to the effect that you—"
He turned his head and looked about him to make absolutely sure that he and the druggist were alone in the tiny prescription pharmacy. The druggist was a gnome-like gnarled little man who could have been any age from fifty to a hundred. They were alone, but Sangstrom dropped his voice just the same. "—to the effect that you have a completely undetectable poison."

The druggist nodded. He came around the counter and locked the front door of the shop, then walked toward a doorway behind the counter. "I was about to take a coffee break," he said. "Come with me and have a cup."

Sangstrom followed him around the counter and through the doorway to a back room ringed by shelves of bottles from floor to ceiling. The druggist plugged in an electric percolator, found two cups and put them on the table that had a chair on either side of it. He motioned Sangstrom to one of the chairs and took the other himself. "Now," he said. "Tell me. Whom do you want to kill, and why?"

"Does it matter?" Sangstrom asked. "Isn't it enough that I pay for—"

The druggist interrupted him with an upraised hand. "Yes, it matters. I must be convinced that you deserve what I can give you. Otherwise—" He shrugged.

"All right," Sangstrom said. "The *whom* is my wife. The *why—*" He started the long story. Before he had quite finished the percolator had finished its task and the druggist briefly interrupted to get the coffee for them. Sangstrom finished his story.

The little druggist nodded. "Yes, I occasionally dispense an undetectable poison. I do so freely; I do not charge for it, if I think the case is deserving. I have helped many murderers."

"Fine," Sangstrom said. "Please give it to me, then."

The druggist smiled at him. "I already have. By the time the coffee was ready I had decided that you deserved it. It was, as I said, free. But there is a price for the antidote."

Sangstrom turned pale. But he had anticipated—not this, but the possibility of a double-cross or some form of blackmail. He pulled a pistol from his pocket.

The little druggist chuckled. "You daren't use that. Can you find the antidote"—he waved at the shelves—"among those thousands of bottles? Or would you find a faster, more virulent poison? Or if you think I'm bluffing, that you're not really poisoned, go ahead and shoot. You'll know the answer within three hours when the poison starts to work."

"How much for the antidote?" Sangstrom growled.

"Quite reasonable. A thousand dollars. After all, a man must live. Even if his hobby is preventing murders, there's no reason why he shouldn't make money at it, is there?"

Sangstrom growled and put the pistol down, but within reach, and took out his wallet. Maybe after he had the antidote, he'd still use that pistol. He counted out a thousand dollars in hundred-dollar bills and put it on the table.

The druggist made no immediate move to pick it up. He said: "And one other thing—for your wife's safety and mine. You will write a confession of your intention—your former intention, I trust—to murder your wife. Then you will wait till I go out and mail it to a friend of mine on the homicide detail. He'll keep it as evidence in case you ever *do* decide to kill your wife. Or me, for that matter.

"When that is in the mail it will be safe for me to return here and give you the antidote. I'll get you the paper and pen. . ."

"Oh, one other thing—although I do not absolutely insist on it. Please help spread the word about my undetectable poison, will you? One never knows, Mr. Sangstrom. The life you save, if you have any enemies, just might be your own."

Some people would call the druggist a "champion of justice." Would you agree?

Do you feel this story is realistic or far-fetched? Why?

All the Years of Her Life

BY MORLEY CALLAGHAN

Alfred began to feel that familiar terror growing in him that had been in him every time he had got into trouble.

They were closing the drugstore, and Alfred Higgins, who had just taken off his white jacket, was putting on his coat and getting ready to go home. The little grey-haired man, Sam Carr, who owned the drugstore, was bending down behind the cash register, and when Alfred Higgins passed him, he looked up and said softly, "Just a moment, Alfred. One moment before you go."

The soft, confident, quiet way in which Sam Carr spoke made Alfred start to button his coat nervously. He felt sure his face was white. Sam Carr usually said, "Good night," brusquely, without looking up. In the six months he had been working in the drugstore Alfred had never heard his employer speak softly like that. His heart began to beat so loud it was hard for him to get his breath. "What is it, Mr. Carr?" he asked.

"Maybe you'd be good enough to take a few things out of your pocket and leave them here before you go," Sam Carr said.

"What things? What are you talking about?"

"You've got a compact and a lipstick and at least two tubes of toothpaste in your pocket, Alfred."

"What do you mean? Do you think I'm crazy?" Alfred blustered. His face got red and he knew he looked fierce with indignation. But Sam Carr, standing by the door with his blue eyes shining brightly behind his glasses and his lips moving underneath his grey moustache, only nodded his head a few times, and then Alfred grew very frightened and he didn't know what to say. Slowly he raised his hand and dipped it into his pocket, and with his eyes never meeting Sam Carr's eyes, he took out a blue compact and two tubes of toothpaste and a lipstick, and he laid them one by one on the counter.

"Petty thieving, eh, Alfred?" Sam Carr said. "And maybe you'd be good enough to tell me how long this has been going on."

"This is the first time I ever took anything."

"So now you think you'll tell me a lie, eh? What kind of a sap do I look like, huh? I don't know what goes on in my own store, eh? I tell you you've been doing this pretty steady," Sam Carr said as he went over and stood behind the cash register.

Ever since Alfred had left school he had been getting into trouble wherever he worked. He lived at home with his mother and his father, who was a printer. His two older brothers were married and his sister had got married last year, and it would have been all right for his parents now if Alfred had only been able to keep a job.

While Sam Carr smiled and stroked the side of his face very delicately with the tips of his fingers, Alfred began to feel that familiar terror growing in him that had been in him every time he had got into trouble.

"I like you," Sam Carr was saying. "I liked you and would have trusted you, and now look what I got to do." While Alfred watched with his alert, frightened blue eyes, Sam Carr drummed with his fingers on the counter. "I don't like to call a cop in point-blank," he was saying as he looked very worried. "You're a fool, and maybe I should call your father and tell him you're a fool. Maybe I should let them know I'm going to have you locked up."

"My father's not home. He's a printer. He works nights," Alfred said.

"Who's at home?"

"My mother, I guess."

"Then we'll see what she says." Sam Carr went to the phone and dialed the number. Alfred was not so much ashamed, but there was the deep fright growing in him, and he blurted out arrogantly, like a strong, full-grown man, "Just a minute. You don't need to draw anybody else in. You don't need to tell her." He wanted to sound like a swaggering, big guy who could look after himself, yet the old, childish hope was in him, the longing that someone at home would come and help him. "Yeah, that's right, he's in trouble," Mr. Carr was saying. "Yeah, your boy works for me. You'd better come down in a hurry." And when he was finished Mr. Carr went over to the door and looked out at the street and watched the people passing in the late summer night. "I'll keep my eye out for a cop," was all he said.

Alfred knew how his mother would come rushing in; she would rush in with eyes blazing, or maybe she would be crying, and she would push him away when he tried to talk to her, and make him feel her dreadful contempt; yet he longed that she might come before Mr. Carr saw the cop on the beat passing the door.

While they waited—and it seemed a long time—they did not speak, and when at last they heard someone tapping on the closed door, Mr. Carr, turning the latch, said crisply, "Come in, Mrs. Higgins." He looked hard-faced and stern.

Mrs. Higgins must have been going to bed when he telephoned, for her hair was tucked in loosely under her hat, and her hand at her throat held her light coat tight across her chest so her dress would not show. She came in, large and plump, with a little smile on her friendly face. Most of the store lights had been turned out and at first she did not see Alfred, who was standing in the shadow at the end of the counter. Yet as soon as she saw him she did not look as Alfred thought she would look: she smiled, her blue eyes never wavered, and with a calmness and dignity that made them forget that her clothes seemed to have been thrown on her, she put out her hand to Mr. Carr and said politely, "I'm Mrs. Higgins. I'm Alfred's mother."

Mr. Carr was a bit embarrassed by her lack of terror and her simplicity, and he hardly knew what to say to her, so she asked, "Is Alfred in trouble?"

"He is. He's been taking things from the store. I caught him red-handed. Little things like compacts and toothpaste and lipsticks. Stuff he can sell easily," the proprietor said.

As she listened Mrs. Higgins looked at Alfred sometimes and nodded her head sadly, and when Sam Carr had finished she said gravely, "Is it so, Alfred?"

"Yes."

"Why have you been doing it?"

"I been spending money, I guess."

"On what?"

"Going around with the guys, I guess," Alfred said.

Mrs. Higgins put out her hand and touched Sam Carr's arm with an understanding gentleness, and speaking as though afraid of disturbing him, she said, "If you would only listen to me before doing anything." Her simple earnestness made her shy; her humility made her falter and look away, but in a moment she was smiling gravely again, and she said with a kind of patient dignity, "What did you intend to do, Mr. Carr?"

"I was going to get a cop. That's what I ought to do."

"Yes, I suppose so. It's not for me to say, because he's my son. Yet I sometimes think a little good advice is the best thing for a boy when he's at a certain period in his life," she said.

Alfred couldn't understand his mother's quiet composure, for if they had been at home and someone had suggested that he was going to be arrested, he knew she would be in a rage and would cry out against him. Yet now she was standing there with that gentle, pleading smile on her face, saying, "I wonder if you don't think it would be better just to let him come home with me. He looks a big fellow, doesn't he? It takes some of them a long time to get any sense," and they both stared at Alfred, who shifted away with a bit of light shining for a moment on his thin face and the tiny pimples over his cheekbone.

But even while he was turning away uneasily Alfred was realizing that Mr. Carr had become aware that his mother was really a fine woman; he knew that Sam Carr was puzzled by his mother, as if he had expected her to come in and plead with him tearfully, and instead he was being made to feel a bit ashamed by her vast tolerance. While there was only the sound of the mother's soft, assured voice in the store, Mr. Carr began to nod his head encouragingly at her. Without being alarmed, while being just large and still and simple and hopeful, she was becoming dominant there in the dimly lit store. "Of course, I don't want to be harsh," Mr. Carr was saying, "I'll tell you what I'll do. I'll just fire him and let it go at that. How's that?" and he got up and shook hands with Mrs. Higgins, bowing low to her in deep respect.

There was such warmth and gratitude in the way she said, "I'll never forget your kindness," that Mr. Carr began to feel warm and genial himself.

"Sorry we had to meet this way," he said. "But I'm glad I got in touch with you. Just wanted to do the right thing, that's all," he said.

"It's better to meet like this than never, isn't it?" she said. Suddenly they clasped hands as if they liked each other, as if they had known each other a long time. "Good night, sir," she said.

"Good night, Mrs. Higgins. I'm truly sorry," he said.

The mother and son walked along the street together, and the mother was taking a long, firm stride as she looked ahead with her stern face full of worry. Alfred was afraid to speak to her, he was afraid of the silence that was between them, so he only looked ahead too, for the excitement and relief was still pretty strong in him; but in a little while, going along like that in silence made him terribly aware of the strength and the sternness in her; he began to wonder what she was thinking of as she stared ahead so grimly; she seemed to have forgotten that he walked beside her; so when they were passing under the Sixth Avenue elevated and the rumble of the train seemed to break the silence, he said in his old, bluster-way, "Thank God it turned out like that. I certainly won't get in a jam like that again."

"Be quiet. Don't speak to me. You've disgraced me again and again," she said bitterly.

"That's the last time. That's all I'm saying."

"Have the decency to be quiet," she snapped. They kept on their way, looking straight ahead.

When they were at home and his mother took off her coat, Alfred saw that she was really only half-dressed and she made him feel afraid again when she said, without even looking at him, "You're a bad lot. God forgive you. It's one thing after another and always has been. Why do you stand there stupidly? Go to bed, why don't you?" When he was going, she said, "I'm going to make myself a cup of tea. Mind, now, not a word about tonight to your father."

While Alfred was undressing in his bedroom, he heard his mother moving around the kitchen. She filled the kettle and put it on the stove. She moved a chair. And as he listened there was no shame in him, just wonder and a kind of admiration of her strength and repose. He could still see Sam Carr nodding his head encouragingly to her; he could hear her talking simply and earnestly, and as he sat on his bed he felt a pride in her strength. "She certainly was smooth," he thought. "Gee, I'd like to tell her she sounded swell."

And at last he got up and went along to the kitchen and when he was at the door he saw his mother pouring herself a cup of tea. He watched and he didn't move. Her face, as she sat there, was a frightened, broken face utterly unlike the face of the woman who had been so assured a little while ago in the drugstore. When she reached out and lifted the kettle to pour hot water in her cup, her hand trembled and the water splashed on the stove. Leaning back in the chair, she sighed and lifted the cup to her lips, and her lips were groping loosely as if they would never reach the cup. She swallowed the hot tea eagerly, and then she straightened up in relief, though her hand holding the cup still trembled. She looked very old.

It seemed to Alfred that this was the way it had been every time he had been in trouble before, that this trembling had really been in her as she hurried out half-dressed to the drugstore. He understood why she had sat alone in the kitchen the night his young sister had kept repeating doggedly that she was getting married. Now he felt all that his mother had been thinking of as they walked along the street together a little while ago. He watched his mother, and he never spoke, but at that moment his youth seemed to be over; he knew all the years of her life by the way her hand trembled as she raised the cup to her lips. It seemed to him that this was the first time he had ever looked upon his mother.

Alfred was surprised at his mother's behaviour in the store. Were you? Do you think she did the right thing?

Do you know anyone like Alfred? What advice would you give him/her?

The Cat

BY NICK MITCHELL

The house seemed to be floating. Oligarski recognized nothing of the land that he knew so well. It was as if he had landed on another planet.

It had been a bad year for Oligarski. He was almost sixty and had lived through enough years to know a bad one when it came along. Three years in a row had been bad for him, but that last one had been the worst, maybe because it was a culmination. It had been like a nail in his coffin.

He took off his cap with the Versatile logo on it, and wiped his brow. He stood on the front porch of his house. The water came up right to the first step. The basement of the house was completely filled. Oligarski was the third generation of his family. His grandfather had homesteaded this section of land near Fisher Branch, cleared the trees and the rocks, and farmed it. His father had stayed on the farm. Oligarski remembered little of his grandfather. The old man used to bounce him up and down on the end of his foot.

Far in the distance, from a cluster of trees, came the "mew" that had sounded all night whenever the wind blew in the direction of the house. It had kept his daughter awake. How the cat had reached the trees was beyond him. But as he stood on the porch and looked more carefully into the distance, he saw a meandering path of snow that explained it. Not all the snow had melted, though most of it would be gone by this afternoon. He looked up at the sun. It looked like it would be the warmest day so far this year.

He had on his rubber wading boots. Though he knew his land like the back of his hand, the half-metre or so of water that covered the fields as far as the eye could see was enough to throw him into confusion. There were ditches and ridges, but now everything was neatly covered by the smooth, still, grey water. If he ventured out in a straight line for the cat, he knew approximately where there was a ditch, but if he misjudged it by even a few centimetres, he would end up head first in the water. He hesitated, not sure what to do.

"Are you going for the cat?" called his wife, from the kitchen.

"In a minute," he called back. He could not disguise his irritation. Here he was, about to lose his farm, and the only thing on anyone's mind was the cat. The last two years, there had been too much rain, and most of the grain had rotted. And from the looks of it this year, it might even be too wet to seed.

Oligarski was of Ukrainian-Polish descent. His grandfather had been Polish. His grandmother, Ukrainian. He came from a hardy breed of farmers and did not want to throw in the towel. But things had become very difficult for him lately. He was having as much difficulty coping with change as with his inability to make a dollar. His son had recently decided to leave the farm and go to the city to find a job. In many ways this had been the straw to break the camel's back. Oligarski had been willing to put up with incredible hardship to grapple with bankruptcy, if only at the back of his mind was the certainty that there was a reason for his struggle. The unspoken reason that had driven him the last few years despite all setbacks, was that his son would take over the farm. But then one day his son had pointed out to him that he did not want a farm that was constantly on the brink of bankruptcy, that could not turn a profit. And when Oligarski thought about it a bit, he saw that his son was right. It was ridiculous to pass along such a burden to his child.

"Ma!" said Caroline. "He still hasn't gone!"

Oligarski turned around and looked at his thirteen-year-old daughter. She was looking at him resentfully, as if he was torturing her cat.

Oligarski stepped off the porch, but almost immediately felt his rubber boot sink into soft mud. He withdrew onto the porch again. Though there was only about thirty centimetres of water, there was pure mud underneath it. The cat mewed in the distance, as if calling him.

Caroline stared at him impatiently. She had wanted him to go out and retrieve the cat by moonlight. He wondered now why he had not done just that. At least he would have got some sleep. As it was, between the cat crying all night, and his daughter tossing restlessly in her bed, no one had slept.

He looked at the strip of snow that rose above the water. The cat had had the brains to use this to get to the trees, but it didn't have the brains to use it to get back. Oligarski stepped off the porch, just as his wife appeared. He took several sticky steps through the water, then climbed onto the snow.

"There!" said his wife, to his daughter. "You see! There's nothing to worry about. Dad will have kitty back here in no time."

Nothing to worry about, thought Oligarski. She had nothing to worry about. He balanced on the snow as it slid out from under his rubber boots. The rubber was slippery on the snow, and he soon found himself on all fours, clinging so as not to fall into the water. Ahead of him the cat cried loudly as if it knew rescue was imminent and was encouraging him, while behind him his daughter called, "Hurry up, daddy! I think the cat's sick!"

This was some game for a man whose world was about to collapse around him. No wonder his father had lost his memory in the last few years of his life. Things were crazy, and it was easier not to remember all your troubles. The old man would just wander away from the farm, forget all about coming home. The neighbours caught on after a time. They would phone if they saw the old man wandering too far from home. Oligarski would drive out and pick him up in the truck.

He fell down on all fours again to keep from slipping into the water. As he looked back, to his surprise he saw that the snow bank he had been using had disappeared. He had mashed it down with his boots and enough of it had crumbled and disappeared under the water so that there would be no way to return unless he waded through the water in the field. He would probably drown the cat, and his daughter would never forgive him. Of course, if he drowned himself at the same time, she just might find it in her heart to think kindly of her father. As he came to his feet again he wondered if, near the end, his memory would go the way it had done with his father. It might be best that way.

He looked at the thin strip of snow between him and the trees. His son had already left for the city. He would find a job for the summer and attend university in the fall. Oligarski did not blame the boy. If he had had a chance himself, he might have left the farm. But the opportunity had never come up. At that time they had been more isolated on the farm with no radio or television. Oligarski had never had much of a chance to consider a career of any kind. He knew the farm from the time he was old enough to help his father shovel grain. He had lived it and breathed it ever since he could remember. He knew every metre of ground on this land. And somehow this knowledge had led him to believe that his son would take over and carry on the tradition of the family. Why he had confused things in this way, he did not understand.

When he reached the cluster of trees, he reached for the branches and hauled himself up onto one of the boughs. The cat was in the tree next to him. There was still the task of getting it down without getting his eyes scratched out. He looked back at the house. It was a modern two-storey, the kind that you would find in a suburb of the city. It had all the conveniences of city life. Except for the isolation, there was nothing lacking.

Oligarski looked for the path of snow he had followed, but there was absolutely nothing to be seen. It was all gone; only the flat, even surface of the water met his eye. He turned and looked in the other direction. Water covered everything as far as the eye could see. In the distance, trees looked like they were growing in it. Though there was no more than thirty centimetres of water in the shallowest spots, it looked to him as if he was in the middle of a lake. The house seemed to be floating. He recognized nothing of the land that he knew so well. It was as if he had landed on another planet.

He rested for a while in the tree. He could hear his daughter calling from the house. There would be no rest for him until he retrieved the cat. He lowered himself into the water and using branches for handholds, manoeuvered himself to the next tree where the orange and white cat sat.

It was some kind of Persian, a stray that had wandered into the farmyard one day. They had enough cats in the barn already, but this one had become Caroline's favourite. It had caught her eye. Oligarski had never seen an orange cat before. It looked exotic. Caroline quickly invented a history for it to make it different from the others and this was excuse enough to bring it into the house, a privilege none of the others ever received. As Oligarski reached up to take it from the branch, it mewed loudly and huddled, puffed up, waiting to see what he would do.

After the water went down and land reappeared again, it just would not be the same farm he had known. The ditches would still be there, the dips, and the gullies. But, despite the detail, it would be different. He would not be able to look upon it as the family farm that his son would take over. Exactly in what light it would appear to him, he was not sure. The water covered the land like wrapping paper covered a gift. It played tricks on him, making him guess as to what kind of surprise was coming.

When he was a child, he used to shake the gifts under the Christmas tree to try to guess what might be inside. So it was with the present situation. He had been waiting for a clue of some kind, an indication as to how he should look upon his farm when it came out of hiding.

He was thinking about this as he reached up and took hold of the cat by its nape. The cat held onto the branch for a moment with its claws. He pulled it harder and its front feet let go. He pulled still harder and its back feet let go. The cat dangled from its head, awkwardly resigned to the way he carried it. He kept it at arm's length as he made his way back to the larger tree and the bough on which he had rested.

When he reached the bough, he climbed onto it and placed the cat against his shoulder. The cat clung with its claws to his heavy felt jacket. He put his other hand on its head and stroked it. The cat looked at him. It had stopped crying. Oligarski stroked it again. No doubt it was scared and hungry. How could this creature possibly understand all this water? But when Oligarski caught himself comforting the cat by talking to it, he stopped abruptly, took it from his shoulder and put it on a nearby branch. He was getting as silly as his daughter. None of his friends would have bothered even going out to get it. They would have let the creature starve. But none of his friends was in his position. None of his friends were on the brink of starvation the way he was. Somehow this is what had made him feel the plight of the creature and had made him venture out to save it.

How was he to get back though? He looked at the house in the distance. It was too far away for his voice to reach anyone and explain that he was stranded. Maybe if the wind had been blowing in that direction like the night before, it would have been possible. But now all he could do was watch. After a time, he saw his wife join his daughter on the front porch. What could they do to help him? Eventually he would have to step into the water and wade back to the house. How long could he sit in the tree?

His wife and daughter appeared to be discussing something. Then he saw his wife form a megaphone with her hands and call to him. But he could make out nothing of the shout. After a while, his wife disappeared and left his daughter standing alone on the porch. Oligarski leaned back against the trunk of the tree. The sun was bright and the air was becoming warm. A few more minutes, he thought, before he waded into the mud and water. And as he rested, his back against the trunk, he sank into reverie, and finally dozed off.

The warm sun was on his face when he opened his eyes. He did not know how long he had been asleep. It was a wonder that he had not fallen out of the tree. But then he remembered reading that people used to live in trees at one time. He believed it now. As he stirred and sat up straighter, he noticed something strange on the water between the house and the tree. It took him a moment before the image made any sense to him. It was Caroline, on a raft of some kind, pushing herself towards him with a stick. He could not believe his eyes. Then he looked at the cat and saw that the cat had its eye on Caroline and the raft, too. It was all mystifying to him.

As she drew closer, he noticed that the raft was just an old wooden door that had been standing against the back of the house. He had put it there after taking it off its hinges. It had been hard for him to recognize with water coursing over it as Caroline moved towards him. While he and the cat watched in astonishment, his wife appeared on the front porch of the house. She stood frozen for a minute, then began to call and shout and gesture for Caroline to come back. His daughter glanced over her shoulder at the gesticulating figure, then continued to push the raft toward the trees. Oligarski was not sure himself whether he should be angry. But after a minute he began to chuckle to himself.

It was crazy really, this small girl rowing out to save her father. That was exactly what she was doing. He wondered if she would have gone after the cat in the same way, had he refused to go out to save it himself. He considered it for a time while he watched her draw nearer, and then concluded that she would not do something like this for the cat alone. She really was coming out to save him. All the grumbling he had done on his way to the trees paled in the light of this. He had never been sure how his daughter saw him. He knew his son and felt that he knew how he looked upon him. His son's decision to abandon the farm had in one way been a surprise, but in another way had been no surprise at all. Difficult as it was for him to accept his decision, he understood why his son had made it. but his daughter had always been a bit of a mystery to him.

He no longer regretted his decision to come out to get the cat. Had he remained at the house, he would not have made the discovery of how much Caroline cared for him. He wondered if maybe this was the reason he had come to get the cat. To his daughter, the animal was special. Maybe he had come to believe in her stories. Maybe he had needed something out of the ordinary to help him through his difficulties. The usual things he depended upon had all fallen away from him.

He left the tree and waded out a few steps when she drew near. He took hold of the door and helped steer it towards the trees. She looked at him, trying to read his face.

"You're not mad at me for coming, are you?" she said.

"Of course not," he said. "If it wasn't for you, I probably would have sat here for a week, until the water went down."

"Ma's really mad."

"Well, we'll worry about that when we get back."

He reached up into the tree and took the cat down. Caroline held out her hands to receive it. He had a bit of trouble peeling the cat away from the branch, but the cat seemed to recover its composure when it was reunited with his daughter.

"Are you coming on the door?" she asked.

"I'll try," he said. "We'll have to see if it can hold me." He picked himself out of the water by one of the branches, and lowered himself gently onto the door. It sank a bit in the water. "What have you got there?" he asked, looking at the stick in her hand.

"Old broom stick."

"Give it here," he said.

He pushed with the rounded stick, and the door began to glide through the water even though it was riding a few centimetres below the surface.

"I see you put on your rubber boots," he said. "Are your feet dry?"

She nodded that they were.

About halfway to the house, his wife appeared on the front porch again. She stood watching as Oligarski pushed the raft closer to the house. For a time, it looked as if she would say something, but eventually she seemed to tire of the slow progress being made, and disappeared into the house again.

As they neared the house, Oligarski noticed that he was no longer beset with the worry that had plagued him earlier. He no longer worried about how the farm would look to him when the water subsided and the land appeared again. He still felt strange about the flood but his apprehension was gone. It was as if a burden had been lifted from his shoulders. He pushed the end of the broomstick into the mud, and propelled the raft forward. His daughter, holding the cat and stroking it, stood at the end of the raft, swaying with each movement forward. Even his wife seemed to have calmed down. She came out to meet them at the last moment as the raft touched the front porch. She helped Caroline and the cat off, and said nothing. The cat leaped from Caroline's shoulder and bounded into the house.

"And you wanted me to throw this old door away," said Oligarski, as he stepped onto the porch. "I told you it would come in handy one of these days."

What makes Oligarski a "special person"? Would you consider his daughter special, too?

Did you ever take a risk to help someone? What happened?

Goalie

BY RUDY THAUBERGER

No one understands. They believe he's invulnerable, the fans, his teammates. They stare at him blankly while he lies on the ice, white-blind, paralyzed, as his knee or his toe or his hand or his chest or his throat burns.

Nothing pleases him. Win or lose, he comes home angry, dragging his equipment bag up the driveway, sullen eyes staring down, seeing nothing, refusing to see. He throws the bag against the door. You hear him, fumbling with his keys, his hands sore, swollen and cold. He drops the keys. He kicks the door. You open it and he enters, glaring, not at you, not at the keys, but at everything, the bag, the walls, the house, the air, the sky.

His clothes are heavy with sweat. There are spots of blood on his jersey and on his pads. He moves past you, wordless, pulling his equipment inside, into the laundry room and then into the garage. You listen to him, tearing the equipment from the bag, throwing it. You hear the thump of heavy leather, the clatter of plastic, the heavy whisper of damp cloth. He leaves and you enter. The equipment is everywhere, scattered, draped over chairs, hung on hooks, thrown on the floor.

You imagine him on the ice: compact, alert, impossibly agile and quick. Then you stare at the equipment: helmet and throat protector, hockey pants, jersey, chest and arm protectors, athletic supporter, knee pads and leg pads, blocker, catching glove and skates. In the centre of the floor are three sticks, scattered, their broad blades chipped and worn. The clutter is deliberate, perhaps even necessary. His room is the same, pure chaos, clothes and magazines everywhere, spilling out of dresser drawers, into the closet. He says he knows where everything is. You imagine him on the ice, focused, intense, single-minded. You understand the need for clutter.

When he isn't playing, he hates the equipment. It's heavy and awkward and bulky. It smells. He avoids it, scorns it. It disgusts him. Before a game, he gathers it together on the floor and stares at it. He lays each piece out carefully, obsessively, growling and snarling at anyone who comes too close. His mother calls him a gladiator, a bullfighter. But you know the truth, that gathering the equipment is a ritual of hatred, that every piece represents, to him, a particular variety of pain.

There are black marks scattered on the white plastic of his skates. He treats them like scars, reminders of pain. His glove hand is always swollen. His chest, his knees, and his biceps are always bruised. After a hard game, he can barely move. "Do you enjoy it?" you ask, "Do you enjoy the game at least? Do you like playing?" He shrugs. "I love it," he says.

Without the game, he's miserable. He spends his summers restless and morose, skating every morning, lifting weights at night. He juggles absent-mindedly; tennis balls, coins, apples, tossing them behind his back and under his leg, see-sawing two in one hand as he talks on the phone, bouncing them off walls and knees and feet. He plays golf and tennis with great fervour, but you suspect, underneath, he is indifferent to these games.

As fall approaches, you begin to find him in the basement, cleaning his skates, oiling his glove, taping his sticks. His hands move with precision and care. You sit with him and talk. He tells you stories. This save. That goal. Funny stories. He laughs. The funniest stories are about failure: the goal scored from centre ice, the goal scored on him by his own defenceman, the goal scored through a shattered stick. There is always a moral, the same moral every time. "You try your best and you lose."

He starts wearing the leg pads in September. Every evening, he wanders the house in them, wearing them with shorts and a T-shirt. He hops in them, does leg lifts and jumping jacks. He takes them off and sits on them, folding them into a squat pile to limber them up. He starts to shoot a tennis ball against the fence with his stick.

As practices begin, he comes home overwhelmed by despair. His skill is an illusion, a lie, a magic trick. Nothing you say reassures him. You're his father. Your praise is empty, invalid.

The injuries begin. Bruises. Sprains. His body betrays him. Too slow. Too clumsy. His ankles are weak, buckling under him. His muscles cramp. His nose bleeds. A nerve in his chest begins to knot and fray. No one understands. They believe he's invulnerable, the fans, his teammates. They stare at him blankly while he lies on the ice, white-blind, paralyzed, as his knee or his toe or his hand or his chest or his throat burns.

To be a goalie, you realize, is to be an adult too soon, to have too soon an intimate understanding of the inevitability of pain and failure. In the backyard, next to the garage, is an old garbage can filled with broken hockey sticks. The blades have shattered. The shafts are cracked. He keeps them all, adding a new one every two weeks. You imagine him, at the end of the season, burning them, purging his failure with a bonfire. But that doesn't happen. At the end of the season, he forgets them and you throw them away.

You watch him play. You sit in the stands with his mother, freezing, in an arena filled with echoes. He comes out without his helmet and stick, skating slowly around the rink. Others move around him deftly. He stares past them, disconnected, barely awake. They talk to him, call his name, hit his pads lightly with their sticks. He nods, smiles. You know he's had at least four cups of coffee. You've seen him, drinking, prowling the house frantically.

As the warm-up drills begin, he gets into the goal casually. Pucks fly over the ice, crashing into the boards, cluttering the net. He skates into the goal, pulling on his glove and blocker. He raps the posts with his stick. No one seems to notice, even when he starts deflecting shots. They come around to him slowly, firing easy shots at his pads. He scoops the pucks out of the net with his stick. He seems bored.

You shiver as you sit, watching him. You hardly speak. He ignores you. You think of the cost of his equipment. Sticks, forty dollars. Glove, one hundred and twenty. Leg pads, thirteen hundred dollars. The pads have patches. The glove is soft, the leather eaten away by his sweat.

The game begins, casually, without ceremony. The scoreboard lights up. The ice is cleared of pucks. Whistles blow. After the stillness of the

face-off, you hardly notice the change, until you see him in goal, crouched over, staring.

You remember him in the backyard, six years old, standing in a ragged net, wearing a parka and a baseball glove, holding an ordinary hockey stick, sawed off at the top. The puck is a tennis ball. The ice is cement. He falls down every time you shoot, ignoring the ball, trying to look like the goalies on TV. You score, even when you don't want to. He's too busy play-acting. He smiles, laughs, shouts.

You buy him a mask. He paints it. Yellow and black. Blue and white. Red and blue. It changes every month, as his heroes change. You make him a blocker out of cardboard and leg pads out of foam rubber. His mother makes him a chest protector. You play in the backyard, every evening, taking shot after shot, all winter.

It's hard to recall when you realize he's good. You come to a point where he starts to surprise you snatching the ball out of the air with his glove, kicking it away with his shoe. You watch him one Saturday, playing with his friends. He humiliates them, stopping everything. They shout and curse. He comes in frozen, tired and spellbound. "Did you see?" he says.

He learns to skate, moving off of the street and onto the ice. The pain begins. A shot to the shoulder paralyzes his arm for ten minutes. You buy him pads, protectors, thinking it will stop the pain. He begins to lose. Game after game. Fast reflexes are no longer enough. He is suddenly alone, separate from you, miserable. Nothing you say helps. Keep trying. Stop. Concentrate. Hold your stick blade flat on the ice.

He begins to practice. He begins to realize that he is alone. You can't help him. His mother can't help him. That part of his life detaches from you, becoming independent, free. You fool yourself, going to his games, cheering, believing you're being supportive, refusing to understand that here, in the rink, you're irrelevant. When you're happy for him, he's angry. When you're sad for him, he's indifferent. He begins to collect trophies.

You watch the game, fascinated. You try to see it through his eyes. You watch him. His head moves rhythmically. His stick sweeps the ice and chops at it. When the shots come, he stands frozen in a crouch. Position is everything, he tells you. He moves, the movement so swift it seems to strike you physically. How does he do it? How? You don't see the puck, only his movement. Save or goal, it's all the same.

You try to see the game through his eyes, aware of everything, constantly alert. It's not enough to follow the puck. The position of the puck is old news. The game. You try to understand the game. You fail.

He seems unearthly, moving to cut down the angle, chopping the puck with his stick. Nothing is wasted. You can almost feel his mind at work, watching, calculating. Where does it come from, you wonder, this strange mind? You try to move with him, watching his eyes through his cage, and his hands. You remember the way he watches games on television, cross-legged, hands fluttering, eyes seeing everything.

Suddenly you succeed, or you think you do. Suddenly, you see the game, not as a series of events, but as a state, with every moment in time potentially a goal. Potentiality. Probability. These are words you think of afterwards. As you watch, there is only the game, pressing against you, soft now, then sharp, then rough, biting, shocking, burning, dull, cold. No players. Only forces, feelings, the white ice, the cold, the echo, all joined. A shot crashes into his helmet. He falls to his knees. You cry out.

He stands slowly, shaking his head, hacking at the ice furiously with his stick. They scored. You never noticed. Seeing the game is not enough. Feeling it is not enough. He wants more, to understand completely, to control. You look out at the ice. The game is chaos again.

He comes home, angry, limping up the driveway, victorious. You watch him, dragging his bag, sticks in his hand, leg pads over his shoulder. You wonder when it happened, when he became this sullen, driven young man. You hear whispers about scouts, rumours. Everyone adores him, adores his skill. But when you see his stiff, swollen hands, when he walks slowly into the kitchen in the mornings, every movement agony, you want to ask him why. Why does he do it? Why does he go on?

But you don't ask. Because you think you know the answer. You imagine him, looking at you and saying quietly, "What choice do I have? What else have I ever wanted to do?"

Did this goalie really have no choice? What advice would you give him?

Does the goalie remind you of anyone you know (maybe yourself)? What do you like about him or her? What do you find hard to accept?

Why doesn't the author give the goalie a name? What effect does that have on you, the reader?

The Good Provider

BY MARION GROSS

Working on the gadget was one thing, but believing that it worked was another. Maybe folks had been right—maybe Omar had gone off his head at last.

Minnie Leggety turned up the walk of her Elm Street bungalow and saw that she faced another crisis. When Omar sat brooding like that, not smoking, not "studying," but just scrunched down inside of himself, she knew enough after forty years to realize that she was facing a crisis. As though it weren't enough just trying to get along on Omar's pension these days, without having to baby him through another one of his periods of discouragement. She forced a gaiety into her voice that she actually didn't feel.

"Why, hello there, Pa, what are you doing out here? Did you have to come up for air?" Minnie eased herself down beside Omar on the stoop and put the paper bag she had been carrying on the sidewalk. Such a little bag, but it had taken most of their week's food budget! Protein, plenty of lean, rare steaks and chops, that's what that nice man on the radio said old folks needed, but as long as he couldn't tell you how to buy it with steak at $1.23 a pound, he might just as well save his breath to cool his porridge. And so might she, for all the attention Omar was paying her. He was staring straight ahead as though he didn't even see her. This looked like one of his real bad spells. She took his gnarled hand and patted it.

"What's the matter, Pa? Struck a snag with your gadget?" The "gadget" filled three full walls of the basement and most of the floor space besides, but it was still a "gadget" to Minnie—another one of his ideas that didn't quite work.

Omar had been working on gadgets ever since they were married. When they were younger, she hotly sprang to his defense against her sisters-in-law: "Well, it's better than liquor, and it's cheaper than pinochle; at least I know where he is nights." Now that they were older, and Omar was retired from his job, his tinkering took on a new significance. It was what kept him from going to pieces like a lot of men who were retired and didn't have enough activity to fill their time and their minds.

"What's the matter, Pa?" she asked again.

The old man seemed to notice her for the first time. Sadly he shook his head. "Minnie, I'm a failure. The thing's no good; it ain't practical. After all I promised you, Minnie, and the way you stuck by me and all, it's just not going to work."

Minnie never had thought it would. It just didn't seem possible that a body could go gallivanting back and forth the way Pa had said they would if the gadget worked. She continued to pat the hand she held and told him soothingly, "I'm not sure but it's for the best, Pa. I'd sure have gotten airsick, or timesick, or whatever it was. What're you going to work on now that you're giving up the time machine?" she asked anxiously.

"You don't understand, Min," the old man said. "I'm through. I've failed. I've failed at everything I've ever tried to make. They always *almost* work, and yet there's always something I can't get just right. I never knew enough, Min, never had enough schooling, and now it's too late to get any. I'm just giving up altogether. I'm through!"

This *was* serious. Pa with nothing to tinker at down in the basement, Pa constantly underfoot, Pa with nothing to keep him from just slipping away like old Mr. Mason had, was something she didn't like to think about. "Maybe it isn't as bad as all that," she told him. "All those nice parts you put into your gadget, maybe you could make us a television or something with them. Land, a television, that would be a nice thing to have."

"Oh, I couldn't do that, Min. I wouldn't know how to make a television; besides, I told you, it almost works. It's just that it ain't practical. It ain't the way I pictured it. Come down, I'll show you." He dragged her into the house and down into the basement.

The time machine left so little free floor space, what with the furnace and coal bin and washtubs, that Minnie had to stand on the stairway while Pa explained it to her. It needed explanation. It had more coloured lights than a pinball machine, more plugs than the Hillsdale telephone exchange, and more levers than one of those newfangled voting booths.

"Now see," he said, pointing to various parts of the machine, "I rigged this thing up so we could move forward or back in time and space both. I thought we could go off and visit foreign spots, and see great things happening, and have ourselves an interesting old age."

"Well, I don't rightly know if I'd have enjoyed that, Pa," Minnie interrupted. "I doubt I'd know how to get along with all them foreigners, and their strange talk and strange ways and all."

Omar shook his head in annoyance. "The Holy Land. You'd have wanted to see the Holy Land, wouldn't you? You could have sat with the crowd at Galilee and listened to the Lord's words right from His lips. You'd have enjoyed that, wouldn't you?"

"Omar, when you talk like that you make the whole thing sound sacrilegious and against the Lord's ways. Besides, I suppose the Lord would have spoke in Hebrew, and I don't know one word of that and you don't either. I don't know but what I'm glad you couldn't get the thing to work," she said righteously.

"But Min, it does work!" Omar was indignant.

"But you said—"

"I never said it don't work. I said it ain't practical. It don't work good enough, and I don't know enough to make it work better."

Working on the gadget was one thing, but believing that it worked was another. Minnie began to be alarmed. Maybe folks had been right—maybe Omar had gone off his head at last. She looked at him anxiously. He seemed all right and, now that he was worked up at her, the depression seemed to have left him.

"What do you mean it works, but not good enough?" she asked him.

"Well, see here," Omar told her, pointing to an elaborate control board. "It was like I was telling you before you interrupted with your not getting along with foreigners, and your sacrilegion and all. I set this thing up to move a body in time and space any which way. There's a globe of the world worked in here, and I thought that by turning the globe and setting these time controls to whatever year you had in mind you could go wherever you had a mind to. Well, it don't work like that. I've been trying it out for a whole week and no matter how I set the globe, no matter how I set the time controls, it always comes out the same. It lands me over at Main and Centre, right in front of Purdey's meat market."

"What's wrong with that?" Minnie asked. "That might be real convenient."

"You don't understand," Omar told her. "It isn't *now* when I get there, it's twenty years ago! That's the trouble, it don't take me none of the places I want to go, just Main and Centre. And it don't take me none of the times I want to go, just twenty years ago, and I saw enough of the Depression so I don't want to spend my old age watching people sell apples. Then on top of that, this here timer don't work." He pointed to another dial. "It's supposed to set to how long you want to stay, wherever you want to go, but it don't work at all. Twenty minutes, and then woosh, you're right back here in the basement. Nothing works like I want it to."

Minnie had grown thoughtful as Omar recounted the faults of the machine. Wasn't it a caution the way even a smart man like Pa, a man smart enough to make a time machine, didn't have a practical bone in his whole sixty-seven-kilogram body? She sat down heavily on the cellar steps and, emptying the contents of her purse on her broad lap, began examining the bills.

"What you looking for, Min?" Omar asked.

Minnie looked at him pityingly. Wasn't it a caution...

Purdey the butcher was leaning unhappily against his chopping block. The shop was clean and shining, the floor was strewn with fresh sawdust, and Purdey himself, unmindful of the expense, had for the sake of his morale donned a fresh apron. But for all that, Purdey wished that he was hanging on one of his chromium-plated meat hooks.

The sky was blue and smogless, something it never was when the shops were operating and employing the valley's five thousand breadwinners. Such potential customers as were abroad had a shabby, threadbare look to them. Over in front of the Bijou old Mr. Ryan was selling apples.

While he watched, a stout, determined-looking woman appeared at the corner of Main and Centre. She glanced quickly around, brushing old Mr. Ryan and his apples with her glance, and then came briskly toward Purdey's shop. Purdey straightened up.

"Afternoon, Ma'am, what can I do for you?" he beamed as though the light bill weren't three months overdue.

"I'll have a nice porterhouse," the lady said hesitantly. "How much is a porterhouse?"

"A dollar a kilogram, best in the house." Purdey held up a beauty, expecting her to change her mind.

"I'll take it," the lady said. "And six lamb chops. I want a rib roast for Sunday, but I can come back for that. No use carrying too much," she explained. "Could you please hurry with that? I haven't very much time."

"New in town?" Purdey asked as he turned to ring up the sale on the cash register.

"Yes, you might say so," the woman said. By the time Purdey turned back to ask her name, she was gone. But Purdey knew she'd be back. She wanted a rib roast for Sunday. "It just goes to show you," Purdey said to himself, surveying the satisfactory tab sticking up from the register, "there still is some money around. Two dollars, and she never even batted an eyelash. It goes to show you!"

———

If you could borrow Minnie's machine, what would you do with your twenty minutes in the past?

What do you think Purdey would do if he knew "the truth"?

What questions would you ask Minnie if you were interviewing her for TV news?

G. Trueheart, Man's Best Friend

Genevieve was a horrible example of what ten years of living with Aunt Prudence would do to any creature. She looked like a pigmy hippopotamus with hair.

Tom Hamilton liked his Aunt Prudence. She taught at the university. Tom's father said she was all brains. Her name was Doctor Prudence Hamilton. When she came to Tom's father's farm in the Cowichan Valley on Vancouver Island, she always brought presents. Tom liked her.

He didn't like her constant companion, Genevieve Trueheart, a dog.

Tom Hamilton was fond of other dogs. He had a dog, a bull terrier called Rusty, a fighter right from the word go. Rusty kept the pheasants out of the garden and the young grain. He worked for a living. Tom couldn't like Genevieve Trueheart. She was good for nothing. She never even looked like a dog. She was a great big soft wheezing lazy wagging monster, a great big useless lump.

Genevieve had been born a Golden Retriever of decent parents and Aunt Prudence had papers to prove it. But Genevieve had eaten so many chocolates and French pastries and frosted cakes that she was three times as wide as a Golden Retriever ought to be. She had the soft muscles of a jellyfish. She couldn't run. She couldn't walk. All she could do was waddle. She was a horrible example of what ten years of living with Aunt Prudence would do to any creature. She looked like a pigmy hippopotamus with hair.

Genevieve Trueheart gave Tom Hamilton a hard time. She followed him. She went wherever he went. She was starved for boys. She never had a chance to meet any in the city. Tom couldn't bend over to tie a boot but her big pink tongue would lick his face. She loved him.

At half-past eight when he finished breakfast and started for school, there on the porch would be Genevieve Trueheart waiting for him.

She wants to go to school with you, Tommy, Aunt Prudence always said.

I think she'd better stay home, Tom always said. It's almost two kilometres. That's too far for her.

Take poor Genevieve, Tommy, Aunt Prudence and his mother always said. You know how she likes being with you.

Tom could have said, Why should I take her? When I take her the kids at school laugh at me. They ask, Why don't you send her back to the zoo and get a dog. But he didn't say that. It would have hurt Aunt Prudence's feelings.

On this morning he thought of something else to say. He said, A friend of mine saw a bear on the road. She had two cubs. We'd better leave Genevieve at home. I'll take Rusty.

Rusty has to stay to chase pheasants, his mother said.

What if I meet a cougar? Tom said.

A fat dog like Genevieve would be a fine meal for a cougar.

Tommy, stop talking, his mother said.

A cougar can pick up a sheep and jump over a fence, Tommy said.

Tom Hamilton, his mother said, get to school!

So Tom Hamilton went down the woodland road with Genevieve Trueheart panting and puffing and snorting behind him. Twice he had to stop while Genevieve sat down and rested. He told her, Rusty doesn't think you're a dog. He thinks you're a big fat balloon that's got a tail and four legs. Tom said, Genevieve, I hope a car comes on the wrong side of the road and gets you, you big fat slob. He never meant it. He said, I hope we meet those bears. He was just talking. He said, Do you know what I'm going to do at lunchtime, Genevieve? I'm going to give the fried pork liver that I have for you to another dog, to any dog who looks like a dog and not like a stuffed mattress, and your chocolate, Genevieve, I'll eat it myself. This was a lie. Tom Hamilton was honest.

Every kid who went to that school came with a dog. Yellow dogs. Brown dogs. Black dogs. White dogs. Black and white dogs. Black, white, and yellow dogs. Black, white, yellow, and brown dogs. They were a happy collection of dogs, and had long agreed among themselves who could beat whom, who could run faster than whom, who had the most fleas. From nine o'clock in the morning until noon they scratched. From noon until one they looked after their owners. From one o'clock until school was out at three they scratched.

These dogs did not welcome Genevieve. They were not jealous because she was a Golden Retriever and had papers to prove it; they didn't believe an animal with a shape like Genevieve was a dog. A Mexican hairless dog, one of those small dogs you can slip into your pocket, put his nose against Genevieve's nose, and what did she do, she rolled over on her back with her feet in the air. After that, there wasn't a dog who would have anything to do with Genevieve Trueheart.

The kids asked Tom, What's she good for?

Tom knew the answer but he never told them. She was good for nothing.

Boy! she's a ball of grease, the kids said.

She's a city dog, Tom said.

Why don't you leave her at home? the kids said.

Because my aunt gives me a dollar a week to walk her to school, Tom said. A lie.

Boy, oh, boy! a kid said, I wouldn't be seen with her for two dollars a week.

After school, Tom waited until all the others had left. He couldn't stand any more unkind words. He took his time going home. He had to. If he hurried, Genevieve would sit down and yelp. They came to the woodland road. It was like a tunnel. The tall trees, the Douglas firs, the cedars, and the hemlocks, all stretched branches over Tom's head. The air seemed cold even in summer. Owls liked the woodland road, and so did tree frogs, and deer liked it when flies were after them, but Tom didn't like it much. He was always glad to get out of it and into the sunshine. Often when he walked along this road he had a feeling things were looking at him. He didn't mind Genevieve too much here. She was company.

This day, Tom knew that something was looking at him. He had the feeling. And there it was!

There it was, all two and a half metres of it, crouched on a rock, above him, a great golden cat, a cougar, a Vancouver Island panther! Its tail was twitching. Its eyes burned green, burned yellow, burned bright. Its ears were flat against its head.

Tom's feet stopped. His blood and all his other juices tinkled into ice, and for a moment the whole world seemed to disappear behind a white wall. A heavy animal brushed against him, and at the shock of that, Tom could see again. It was Genevieve. She had sat down and, to rest herself, was leaning on his leg.

The cougar's ears were still flat, its eyes burning as if lighted candles were in them. It was still crouched on the rock, still ready to spring.

Tom heard a thump, thump, thump, thump, thump, and he thought it was the sound of his heart, but it wasn't. It was Genevieve beating her tail against the gravel to show how happy she was to be sitting doing nothing. That made Tom mad. If she had been any kind of a dog she would have known about the cougar before Tom did. She should have smelled him. She should have been just out of reach of his claws and barking. She should have been giving Tom a chance to run away. That's what Rusty would have done. But no, not Genevieve; all she could do was bump her fat tail and look happy.

The cougar had come closer. A centimetre at a time, still in a crouch, he had slid down the rock. Tom could see the movement in his legs. He was like a cat after a robin.

Tom felt sick, and cold, but his brain was working. I can't run, he

thought, if I run he'll be on me. He'll rip Genevieve with one paw and me with the other. Tom thought, too, that if he had a match he could rip pages from one of his school books and set them on fire for he knew that cougars and tigers and leopards and lions were afraid of anything burning. He had no match because supposing his father had ever caught him with matches in his pocket during the dry season, then wow and wow and wow! Maybe, he thought, if I had a big stone I could stun him. He looked. There were sharp, flat pieces of granite at the side of the road where somebody had blasted.

The cougar jumped. It was in the air like a huge yellow bird. Tom had no trouble leaving. He ran to the side of the road and picked up a piece of granite.

Of course, when he moved, Genevieve Trueheart, who had been leaning against his leg, fell over. She hadn't seen anything. She lay there. She was happy. She looked like a sack of potatoes.

The cougar walked around Genevieve twice as if he didn't believe it. He couldn't tell what she was. He paid no attention to Tom Hamilton. He had seen men before. He had never seen anything like Genevieve. He stretched his neck out and sniffed. She must have smelled pretty good because he sat down beside her and licked one of his paws. He was getting ready for dinner. He was thinking, Boy, oh, boy! this is a picnic.

Tom Hamilton could have run away, but he never. He picked up one of those sharp pieces of granite.

The cougar touched Genevieve with the paw he had been licking, friendly-like, just to know how soft the meat was. Genevieve stopped wagging her tail. She must have thought that the cougar's claws didn't feel much like Tom Hamilton's fingers. She lifted her head and looked behind her. There can be no doubt but that she was surprised.

Tom was ashamed of her. Get up and fight! he yelled. Any other dog would fight. Rusty would have put his nips in before the cougar got finished with the job. But not Genevieve. She rolled over on her back and put her four fat feet in the air. She made noises that never had been heard. She didn't use any of her old noises.

The cougar was disgusted with the fuss Genevieve was making. He snarled. His ears went back. Candles shone in his green-yellow eyes. He slapped Genevieve between his paws like a ball.

Tom saw smears of blood on the road and pieces of Genevieve's hide in the cougar's claws. He still had a chance to run away. He never. He threw the piece of granite. He hit the cougar in its middle. The cougar turned, eyes green, eyes yellow.

How long the cougar looked at Tom, Tom will never know.

The sweet smell of Genevieve's chocolate-flavoured blood was too much for the cougar. He batted her about like a ball again. Tom picked up another piece of granite that weighed almost five kilograms, and bang! he hit the cougar right in the face.

The cougar fell on top of Genevieve. Then the cougar stood up and shook its head. Then it walked backwards like a drunken sailor.

And at that moment a bus full of lumberjacks who were going into town rounded the curve. The tires screeched as the driver stopped it , and thirty big lumberjacks got out yelling like—well, you never heard such yelling, and the cougar quit walking backwards and jumped out of sight between two cedars.

What did Genevieve Trueheart do? That crazy dog waggled on her stomach down the road in the same direction the cougar had gone. She was so scared she didn't know what she was doing.

Boy, oh, boy! that's some dog, the lumberjacks said. She just won't quit. She's a fighter.

Yah! Tom said.

She's bleeding, the lumberjacks said. She saved your life. We'd better get her to a doctor.

They put Genevieve Trueheart and Tom Hamilton in the bus.

Boy, oh, boy! the lumberjacks said, a fighting dog like that is man's best friend.

Yah! Tom said.

The bus went right into Tommy's yard and the thirty lumberjacks told Tommy's mother and father and Aunt Prudence how Genevieve Trueheart, man's best friend, had saved Tommy.

Yah! Tom said.

Then Aunt Prudence put an old blanket and old newspapers over the back seat of her car so the blood wouldn't drip into the fabric when she was taking Genevieve Trueheart to the horse, cow, and dog doctor.

Aunt Prudence said, Now you know how much she loves you, Tommy. She saved your life.

Yah! Tommy said.

Has anyone ever taken the credit (or blame) for something you did? How did it end?

What other weird situations can you imagine Genevieve and Tom getting into?

Golden Pants

BY ROGER LEMELIN

I began to whine my disapproval, "Oh no, mother! Everyone'll make fun of me. I'll look like a church ornament."

My parents were not far from poverty when they had their first child, me. And since I was the first born, I was always older than my brothers. You might take the commonplace wisdom of this remark for a great piece of nonsense, but you will understand its full significance when I tell you that my mother, when she married, did not know how to sew. Seeing the perfect proportions of her magnificent baby Lemelin, however, she decided with my help to start learning immediately. She studied patiently, but she never really mastered the craft.

I became the unhappy guinea pig for her experiments. And the results proved to be truly catastrophic. Trousers, coveralls, shirts, jackets—they were all slightly askew in several details which always made my friends laugh, but which seemed to my mother nothing but minor irregularities in view of the overall harmony of her creations. Just think, she had success-fully made two arms, two legs, two shoulders, and a number of but-tonholes; what matter if they were too long, or too narrow, or different lengths? She was a woman who was sure of herself, mother of a son who later on could boast of the same calm assurance in life, thanks to a pair of golden pants that she made for him at the height of his excruciating timidity.

Even now I shudder to think of those days of public presentation when my mother exposed me before aunts and friends imprisoned in one of her masterpieces. Naturally, when my brothers grew into sizes I had outgrown, they profited from her past errors, for it is fair to say that my mother had a certain critical sense and corrected herself on them. But as for me, since I was the oldest, it was my fate to be "the first by whom the new is tried" each time I reached one of those critical stages when my clothes required new dimensions and a new creative effort. Cutting back on expenses no doubt, mother chose materials for me that would not cause her too much remorse if she wasted them in her first shot at a new coat or pair of trousers. A wave of discomfort still sweeps over me when I remember a certain summer suit fashioned out of an old grey overcoat passed down from my uncle the postman. I twisted and squirmed in it at my school desk like a lice-infested weathercock. Stray horsehairs scratched my neck and tickled my armpits and I had pins and needles all over. My idea of heaven at the time was to be outfitted at Simpsons or Eatons, like the other boys. Often mother got her supplies of material from the sacristy at the parish church. The parish priest, who saw in her an exemplary mother of a large family, would give her old cassocks, worn-out religious banners and all sorts of church linen, all of which was immediately consumed by the maternal sewing factory. I was clothed by the church. But one day an unexpected source of materials was opened to the inexhaustible seamstress.

Two of my uncles arrived from Detroit where they had been laid off by the Chrysler plant. It was the black days of 1931. They opened a garage at Quebec where they hoped to put to use the experience they had gained in the States. They specialized in making over interiors of high-class automobiles. One day a wealthy client brought in his 1920 Cadillac and several days later my uncle came home in triumph with a piece of heavy plush material that had covered the back seat of the car. First my mother nearly fainted; then she fixed me with a look that said, "At last! My boy, your great day has come!" I couldn't believe it. That plush Cadillac upholstery was over half a centimetre thick and once must have been gold coloured. But dust and time had changed its luster to a dowdy brown. With great gusto my mother set to beating the material. Then she brushed it and rebrushed it ambitiously. The more the cloth took on its original sheen,

the more my mother's face shone with pleasure. Then fate struck. Turning toward me, mother said, "Roger, there's a fine pair of pants for you here, and they'll wear like everlasting." She was in her glory. I began to whine my disapproval, "Oh no, mother! Everyone'll make fun of me. I'll look like a church ornament." But mother overruled me with the happy thought that her test model was now in the same class as the Cadillac, a gold one at that, and for a good long time to come.

The golden pants, full and floppy, were finished at 5 p.m. on the twenty-eighth day of May in the month of the Virgin Mary. Mother had me try them on at once. Holy Saints, but they were heavy and hot! I refused to leave the house. I refused even though I heard the shouts of my friends playing ball in the backyard. At supper I had no appetite. I felt as though I had my legs stuck through a couple of feather bolsters instead of a pair of pants. I could see what agony was in store for me. This would be the pinnacle of my humiliation.

Thus I reached the fourteenth Station of the Cross in the painful career of a child who is clothed by a mother who doesn't know how to sew. Until then I had endured the mocking smiles of my schoolmates as I might have put up with a throbbing toothache. Now they would split their sides laughing, and Henri Fontaine would laugh louder than all the rest together.

I lurked in the house all that evening but next day there was nothing for it but to wear the pants to school. Mother mounted guard at the foot of my bed and under her watchful eye I couldn't avoid getting into the golden pants. She was a woman who was determined to see her own ideas triumph, even though she was obliged to go all the way to school with me for fear I might take refuge in the field next door like a wounded animal.

I went into the classroom and reached my seat, overwhelmed by the whispers of my classmates. My place was near the front and Fontaine, who used to copy over my shoulder, sat behind me. The teacher, a just, severe man, began the catechism lesson. He often asked me tricky questions and liked to hold my answers up as an example for the rest of the class.

"Lemelin, when you die will you go to heaven or hell? Stand up."

I got halfway up and stuttered out: "I don't know. It all depends if I die in a state of mortal sin—"

A burst of laughter. Deeply shocked, the teacher fixed me with the withering look a bishop might use on a heretic. I had deceived the hope he had placed in me and I knew he would hold it against me. He went over to write on the blackboard, and as soon as he turned his back, *bang*! a piece of chalk thrown full force hit him on the neck. He turned around slowly and took us all in with an icy stare.

"I want to know right now, who did that?"

At first a leaden silence was all the answer he got. I almost felt like the guilty one myself. Because of my answer to his question on heaven and hell, he couldn't help suspecting me.

"All right," he lashed out at us, "who is it?"

There was a movement in the class and I realized that behind me Henri Fontaine had stood up.

"I know who it was, Sir!"

"Well then, what are you waiting for? Speak out."

"It was Roger Lemelin who wants to show you his golden pants!"

I thought I would die. The class exploded in laughter but the teacher didn't even crack a smile.

"Was it you Lemelin?"

"No—yes—"

I was completely paralyzed; my mind went blank; I didn't have the courage to deny it; he wouldn't have believed me anyway.

"Not surprising you're not so sure of going to heaven," he burst out. "Come up here, and stand facing the blackboard."

He laid hold of a long oak ruler and set to beating me furiously on the buttocks as hard as he could. Usually one stroke of this ruler was enough to start any child howling with pain. O wonderful surprise! I could hardly feel it. The ruler sank into the thick plush and thanks to the air cushion it hardly reached my skin. The teacher, unaware of this phenomenon, redoubled his efforts, flailing me like a madman.

"Ouff! Ouff! Ouff!" he gasped. "Are you going to break down or not? You hard-boiled little brute! You young thug, you!"

I remained unperturbed, even glancing back at my persecutor with a look of embarrassed pity on my face which infuriated him all the more. Then I felt on my back and well-scourged backside a wave of admiration sweeping up toward me from the class.

Suddenly a voice cried out: "Stop, Sir! It wasn't Lemelin, it was Fontaine!"

The teacher, by now pale with exertion, stopped in mid-swing and looked at me with an expression of such deep apology that I will never forget it. Slowly he laid the ruler on his desk, turned me around to face the class, and ordered Fontaine who was shaking in his boots to come forward. The teacher tried to get back his breath and as for me, I didn't know whether I should try to get back to my place or not. I moved off toward my seat.

"No, wait," said the teacher. "I want to ask you another question. Do you want me to beat Fontaine?"

For the first time in my life someone implored me for mercy: my enemy.

"No, Sir."

"Apologize, Fontaine."

"I'm sorry, Roger."

"Now go and sit down. And let this fine gesture be an example of charity and dignity to you."

When the class was over my schoolmates surrounded me like a hero and not one word was said about my golden pants, for deep down children admire courage more than fine clothes. I was famous! I had stood it without flinching, without moving a muscle. I gloried in their admiration, but a vague feeling of guilt began to stir in my heart. Then some of the girls came over and suddenly they began to examine my pants. I broke out in a cold sweat. But I was wrong, they just started twittering with admiration.

The next day, thanks to the spell of golden plush over the fair sex and thanks to its incontestable ruler-proof qualities, all the boys asked their mothers to make them golden pants like Roger Lemelin's.

Since that day I have always been sure of myself, and at the most trying moments in my life I tell myself that I have still got on a pair of golden pants.

In your experience, are people reluctant to appear different? Where do you stand on the subject?

If you had a chance to interview the author, Roger Lemelin, what would you ask him?

Have you ever been seriously embarrassed? How did you feel then? Now?

The Crystal Stars Have Just Begun to Shine

BY MARTHA BROOKS

I wish my father had a girlfriend. It's hell being loved by someone who spends his whole miserable life just looking after you. But he rarely goes out. He is one very drab dude.

Lisa Barnett, moving down the halls, books clasped against her chest, tosses tawny hair away from her eyes in one fluid motion.

How does she do that? Just once I'd like to be able to do that. I have this wild frizzy hair that my boyfriend, Brad, says drives him crazy with unrequited passion, and then he leans me back in his arms and his bicycle topples to the ground. Brad's hair is black with a dyed green stripe down the centre. Brad is half Japanese.

My dad is Jamaican. His hair is more agreeable than mine—always soft, like he's just been caught in the rain. My Mom's hair, I can see in photos, is much like Lisa Barnett's, although it could be any colour now. Who knows? I don't remember her except for the photos. She was young and pretty when she checked out.

A thought strikes! Lisa Barnett could look like my half-sister. The one I've never met.

Daddy is sometimes a terrible yeller and sometimes a hugger. In between times, he's quite reserved. At night, he sits alone in his armchair and watches reruns of *M*A*S*H*. He gets up every morning and goes to a job he hates. He buys the best of everything he can afford for us and has an aversion to leftovers. So I always eat them cold for breakfast before I go to school; this helps ease my sense of guilt.

I feel guilty a lot. I sometimes even feel guilty about that because after he's yelled, when I'm bent over homework and stuffing my face with a snack, he comes up behind me, wraps his arms around my shoulders, and mumbles parental anguish. I'm gumming a mouthful of chips and there he is, rocking me cheek to cheek, telling me I'm all he's got.

It's hell being loved by someone who spends his whole miserable life just looking after you. I wish he had a girlfriend. But he rarely goes out, that's how much of a rut he's in. A couple of years ago I came home from a movie and he and this woman were sitting in the living room, drinking beer, all cuddled up on the couch with the TV blaring. She was a redhead. She smiled at me and I immediately liked her. I was so relieved to see him with somebody. But he was embarrassed. As if a parent, for pete's sake, isn't supposed to have feelings like the rest of us mortals. After that night I didn't see the redhead again. I was so disgusted with him I never asked who she was or where she'd come from.

Brad, my boyfriend, says it's probably just that he's too old now to enjoy women.

"My God," I tell him, "he's only forty-six!"

"So," he shrugs, "let's fix him up with somebody."

"Like who?"

"I dunno. We must know somebody who's as old as him."

Daddy's sparkling social life suggests a handful of possibilities. We start eliminating the implausibles and what remains is Rita, the over-permed check-out lady at Payfair. She looks to be about his age and is friendly, kind, divorced, and available. I have, however, one reservation. She's rather flabby. I feel that if we're going to set my father up with a woman, she's got to be in good shape.

"Why?" says Brad. "I don't see your dad out jogging and he drives a bus all day long."

"He's perfectly fit," I say protectively.

"He's got a paunch," Brad says cruelly, and smiles. He has these marvellous eyebrows, like wings; they move about at will. When he's excited, his whole face looks as if at any moment it'll take off somewhere.

"You have to face facts, Deirdre," he says, leaning over the counter in his mother's kitchen, where we're sitting on high stools as we pig out on

Calamato olives and oatmeal biscuits that Brad himself has made. He plants me with a nice cozy kiss. "Look," he continues, "Rita doesn't exactly make *me* sweat. But who knows what she'll do for your father?"

"Maybe he'd be better off with Auntie Eulie's friend Ginny after all," I muse. "She's better looking. Besides, she's black. A change, they say, is as good as a rest."

"Ginny, as we have already discussed, is wacko," says Brad. "She's desperate and totally unstable. Would you want her for a stepmother?"

In spite of Brad's green hair, he's really a very straight-ahead guy. He thinks all love relationships should end happily in marriage. His Italian mother and Japanese father have been married over twenty-three years. He says from the minute he laid eyes on me he knew we were right for each other. He had his mother work out our astrological signs, and according to the reading ours would be a marriage made in heaven. I told him to quit talking that way, we're only fourteen. He responded, wiggling his eyebrows, "In seven years I'm going to marry you, Deirdre, so don't argue with Destiny."

My father does most of our grocery shopping at Payfair. Sometimes I go with him. He shops every Thursday evening after supper. He makes a list, carefully marking off with a little red tick each of the specials he's seen advertised at other stores. Then he can comparison shop. At the store he checks prices according to units instead of weight. When he shops he looks like the male version of a bag lady. He is one very drab dude. You have to imagine a skinny balding black man (with a *slight* paunch) in a shapeless camel coat (Zellers special, 1979), wine-coloured polyester slacks, and black rubber galoshes.

"You're going to have to do something about the clothes, Deirdre," says Brad. "Doesn't he own anything that looks modern?"

"I gave him jeans for Christmas last year. He never wears them," I say, suddenly discouraged.

"Make him wear the jeans Thursday night. And does he own a decent sweater—or anything?"

"Only a navy turtleneck Auntie Eulie gave him to go with the jeans," I say. "He's never worn that either."

Thursday night I make dinner and invite Brad to stay. Daddy gets home and kisses my forehead and asks Brad if he's ever considered dying his green stripe orange. He laughs all the way to the bathroom, where he washes up. Then he goes to his bedroom to change. I go and tap lightly on his door. "Daddy," I say, "please don't wear those purple pants tonight."

"What's wrong with the purple pants?" he says from behind the door.

"They're so tacky."

"They're perfectly fine, I wear them all the time," he says indignant and ready to yell.

"Exactly," I snap back. "And I get tired of looking at you in them. It's time you changed your image. Get reckless." Sometimes, if I state my mind firmly enough, he comes through.

Dead silence from behind the door. Then a suspicious, "Why are you all of the sudden so concerned about the way I look?"

"The jeans," I say. "Okay?"

"They're obscenely tight, Deirdre," he says coldly.

"They're supposed to be tight. That's how they're worn. Are you going to wear those purple pants until you drop dead? I'll have to bury you in them."

"All right," he mutters, "all right."

I stay by the door, breathing.

"What else?" he says.

"Else?"

"What else do you want me to wear. With the tight jeans."

"Oh," I say, as casually as possible, "well, what about that nice sweater Auntie Eulie gave you?"

Another silence.

"It itches," he whines.

"Wear an undershirt," I say, and quickly leave.

He appears, five minutes later, looking uncomfortable and handsome.

Brad stares at him, obviously amazed. Daddy gives him the cold eye and flares up. "What're you gawking at? It's my fashion statement."

"Terrific," says Brad. Later, in the car, he whispers out of the corner of his mouth, "For God's sake make sure he takes off that coat when we get there."

Rita smiles warmly as we trail snow through the door. She doesn't appear to be busy tonight. She's running through a litre of milk for an old lady with an English accent.

"Hi Rita!" Brad and I say, almost in unison. Daddy scurries off to get his cart. He hasn't even acknowledged her.

"Love in bloom," says Brad sarcastically, as we traipse after Daddy.

"I'll attend to his coat," I say, ignoring this. "Your job is the candies."

In the produce section Daddy pauses over bags of celery. He lifts several, checking each for weight. Light celery is stringy, heavy celery is succulent. He frowns, decides against buying celery this week, and moves on to the broccoli, where he scrutinizes the heads through his half glasses. Brad has disappeared. I imagine him whisking back down Aisle 2 so he'll come out directly in front of Rita's till. Now, he's reaching into his jacket. He produces a heart-shaped box of chocolates he bought earlier in the day at the drugstore. It didn't look too fresh, but what can you do? This is November and they're probably a holdover from last Valentine's day. But the heart shape was absolutely essential, you see, because older ladies really like that kind of stuff.

"They sure keep this store hot, don't they?" I say to Daddy.

"Huh?" He's carefully shaking out a plastic produce bag.

"Want me to hold your coat?"

"Why would I want you to hold my coat?" He eases two stalks of broccoli into the bag.

I see I'm going to have to be more forceful. "Daddy, for heaven's sake, you look like a bag lady in that coat. What will people think? Do you want to embarrass me?"

He takes off his glasses, waves them impatiently around.

"Deirdre, what on earth are you talking about? What people? Do you see any people in this store? There are no people. None."

"Well...there could be. There might be. *Anybody* could walk through that door, right now."

"Tsk!" says Daddy, scowling. But he unbuttons the coat before moving on to the apples. His sweater and jeans are at least visible.

Brad slips up behind me just as we progress to the canned goods.

"That took long enough," I whisper tensely.

We hang back like a couple of thieves. Daddy is checking out the canned tomatoes.

"She's terrific!" says Brad, eyebrows poised for lift-off. "I mean, up until now I must admit I've totally overlooked her personality and her eyes. She's got great eyes! But if I was an older man—yeah! I'd take a chance on her myself."

"I want to know her reaction, Brad."

"Shock."

"Good or bad?" I say, watching his face carefully.

"At first it was hard to tell. She just froze with this blank expression. I then told her he was too shy to give them to her himself but that she could thank him personally when she rang up his groceries."

"What'd she say?"

"Nothing. Believe it or not, she smiled like she'd just been handed a ticket to Florida. Your father has something I've missed." He waves at Daddy who, cautious, still scowling, holds aloft a large can of stewed tomatoes.

"I don't see why you're so surprised," I say haughtily. One down. One to go. Please God, let him be smiling when he gets to Rita's till. If you do, I'll eat cold pork every morning for the next month.

Fifteen minutes before closing, Daddy has finally put the last item in his cart. He wheels over to Rita's till. She nods and smiles enigmatically.

"Evening Rita," he says, throwing down a large tub of Monarch margarine.

She rings it through. I notice she's freshly applied dark pink lipstick. My father makes a remark about the weather and stares dismally past her shoulder out the window at the snow that is singing against the glass.

Wordlessly, Rita rings through the rest of the groceries. I've never noticed how much better she looks up close than far away. Up close you really *can* see that her best feature is her eyes. They're pale amber with thick lashes. Her nose is perhaps too big, her skin sort of saggy. But those eyes! She really talks with them. Too bad all this seems to be lost on Daddy. If he'd only look directly at her he'd see what's there.

Just when I think we're never going to get this show on the road, she rings up the bill and, as Daddy hands her three twenty-dollar bills, sort of leans into him and whispers, practically in his ear, "Thanks for the box of chocolates, Elliot. It really made my day."

Daddy doesn't move. He seems paralyzed, except for his eyes, which shift upward to her, back to us, then dart wildly about the store as he processes this information. Finally he takes off his glasses, seems about to say something, and can't. He looks back at her, smiles. She smiles back. Her eyes do a bit of talking. Daddy's eyes start doing their own talking.

I never knew this would be so embarrassing! I can't watch them anymore so I turn around to Brad who still is. Mesmerized, he wears a foolish smile.

I wish somebody would say something out loud. Nobody does. Eventually we leave, each holding onto bags of groceries. Our warm breath hits the outside air and searches out the night. Overhead the crystal stars have just begun to shine.

—

Do you think that Deirdre's view of her father is accurate? Does she exaggerate?

What is the funniest incident you've experienced with an adult? Record it in your Writer's Notebook.

The Secluded Lot

BY ELIZABETH MORISON TOWNSHEND

Then it was that Mr. Jerome began to understand. The full implications left him aghast. There was no precedent for this in all cemetery history!

"I'd like to inquire about a lot," the old man said, the effort of decision evident in his voice. "At my age you never know...."

"It's a good investment," Mr. Jerome replied. Through years of experience he knew these rather delicate matters must be handled with a businesslike approach. "Lots have gone up a good third in value over the past few years. That is, if you ever wanted to resell."

"No, I won't want to resell."

Mr. Jerome looked at the old man thoughtfully. The old-timer was difficult to bracket. *Don't be fooled by the frayed cuffs,* he told himself, *there's probably more life-savings under his mattress than most people have in the bank.*

"This section was just opened up last year," he said, pointing to the large map on the wall. It might have been any map in any real estate office, except for the heading. The dreaded title was blazoned forth:

REST HAVEN CEMETERY

"I'd prefer an older location." The old man looked down at his unpolished shoes, embarrassed. "I mean, where trees and shrubs have had a chance to grow."

"We've still a few left in the older sections—at various price ranges. The Avenue lots are more expensive, of course."

"Too much traffic," the old man said.

"There's one or two on Ridge Road and Cypress Hill—exclusive areas, many old families up there."

"I'd like a good view," the old man explained. "but more important, privacy."

"That will run the price up," Mr. Jerome warned. He was not sure how much price mattered.

"Haven't you something out of the way, sort of hard to find? I don't want relatives interfering—nosing about, you know."

Mr. Jerome studied the map thoughtfully. The blacked-in marks indicated which plots had been sold and occupied. With the exception of the new areas, there were few white vacancies left.

"There might be room for just one more off Willow Walk here," he said. "Needs a bit of clearing, though, and a proper entrance. It would be very private."

"Just the one?"

"Yes."

"Then I think I'd like to see it—if you have the time."

Mr. Jerome looked at his watch: "Yes, I will have the time."

"The size?"

"A little bigger than standard: one by two and a half metres—sets off the headstone just right."

They entered a black limousine and drove slowly through the cemetery. The shade trees stretched their branches over the consecrated ground. A warbler began its plaintive melody. Others joined the chant, until a veritable choir filled the air. Through the open window came the fragrant smells of spring. Here were splashes of brilliant pink azaleas, extravagant dogwoods, forsythia with weeping golden blossoms. They passed prim beds of narcissi and tulips, clumps of bleeding-heart, drifts of pansies and forget-me-nots among the low-growing evergreens.

"Spring is kind of a promise," the old man was saying, obviously moved.

All winter Mr. Jerome, the head gardener and the men at the greenhouse had planned and anticipated just this impression. Now it all seemed so spontaneous and natural—worth hiring the extra clippers and cutters, seeders and transplanters. Yes, Mr. Jerome was pleased.

Where Willow Walk circled downhill again, the limousine came to a halt. Mr. Jerome guided the old man between chiselled, high-polish marbles, between tall and rectangular shafts of granite.

"That's Carrara marble," Mr. Jerome informed him. "This is Vermont. Nice colour, that rose—specially imported Aberdeen granite—about the most durable there is." Carefully circling a slightly raised mound, Mr. Jerome continued: "Now don't let them fool you on synthetics—that new cement and marble chip mix—it won't hold up at all."

Parting the branches of the heavy thicket, Mr. Jerome led the way. Against a natural crag was just room for a bigger than standard lot. Covered with a tangle of unruly vines and underbrush, it was obviously an afterthought.

"Well, here we are," Mr. Jerome said brightly. It was in far worse condition than he remembered and quite inaccessible. Besides, a bramble had caught on the sleeve of his good suit and left a slight tear.

"Of course, it needs a little fixing."

"No, I like it the way it is—wild and secret and uncared-for—hidden by the thicket of branches."

For some time, the old man stood there, gazing off into the distance. "Am I allowed..." he hesitated, correcting himself. "Is the purchaser allowed to visit it at any time?"

"Come as often as you like," Mr. Jerome adjusted his black tie. "Perpetual care, you know, is included in the purchase price."

"I don't want perpetual care." The old gentleman was indignant. "As if you could make promises for the next generation and the next. I mean, with atomic and hydrogen bombs and goodness knows what else."

"Then in that case, we could give you a special price."

In Mr. Jerome's language this meant the highest possible figure at which the customer would buy. Shrewdly, he estimated the demand, the desire and upped the figure ten per cent.

"It's higher than I thought," the old man said sadly. "But it's just what I wanted."

"Then why not take it?" Mr. Jerome was an expert in these matters. "After all, it's for eternity."

"And eternity," the old man added, "is kind of a long time."

"Then it's settled." Mr. Jerome hastened to close the deal. "The contract can be worded to accord with your wishes."

"My last wishes," the old man said.

Mr. Jerome was glad to be back in the safety of his mahogany office again. Carefully he crossed out the *Perpetual Care* clause and instructed his secretary, Miss Jones, to type in the old man's name on the blank lines between the small print—*Mortimer Blake*.

The old man adjusted his glasses, but the print was obviously too fine for him to read.

"No loans or mortgages may be raised on a burial lot, you understand—nor can they be seized for debt." Mr. Jerome recited the routine clauses with a let's-be-done-with-it indifference.

Waiting, embarrassed, the old man glanced at the file clerk—sorting a large stack of documents and correspondence. This particular one had her puzzled. Undecided, she slipped it into a box marked "Pending," and the old man wondered what, under the circumstances, *pending* might mean.

"Please sign here." Mr. Jerome pushed the document towards him. The old man signed in a shaky hand.

"Good afternoon, Rest Haven." Miss Jones used just the right intonation over the telephone. "Services tomorrow at eleven in the chapel."

The telephone rang again. "It's about that advertisement in the *Herald*, sir."

Mr. Jerome picked up the receiver. "The same ad—just a gentle reminder," he said, "and the usual space."

Slowly old Mr. Blake counted out his money. Yes he had brought the entire sum in cash. Between phone calls, Mr. Jerome made out a receipt and handed him his copy. "Good morning, Rest Haven," the efficient Miss Jones was saying. Then her voice took on that tone of practised solemnity: "One minute, please..."

Fumbling with his hat, the old man started for the door.

During the ensuing year old man Blake made periodic visits to his lot. All the workmen in the cemetery knew him by name. But in this separate little world, where personal feelings were respected, nobody thought it odd that he went quite regularly to commune with nature and the life everlasting.

As a cortège neared Willow Walk, Mr. Jerome could see the old man in the distance, parting the bushes and disappearing from view. After the Committal Service—when everything possible had been done for the Departed and the Bereaved had gone their sorrowful ways—something prompted Mr. Jerome to intrude on the old man's privacy—perhaps a word or two of comfort, which he knew so well how to administer.

On the other side of the thicket he was surprised to find Mr. Blake stooping over a high, square, white box, intent on fixing something. A bee circled slowly overhead, then dove for its target.

"Ouch!" yelled Mr. Jerome. "That cursed bee stung me."

"I'm sorry," the old man said, "but that sting cost the bee its life."

Then it was that Mr. Jerome began to understand. The full implications left him aghast. There was no precedent for this in all cemetery history.

"How dare you operate a beehive in this cemetery?"

"It's on my property. I purchased it, did I not?"

"No business such as this is allowed within this sanctuary."

"I'm not soliciting business. The bees are just going about their normal and natural pursuits. Besides, Rose Haven Nectar brings a special price."

"You sell the honey?" Jerome was shocked.

"Maybe it was just beginner's luck," old man Blake replied modestly, "but those twenty-dollar Beginner's Beekeeping Outfits certainly work wonders. Like the advertisement said, I had over forty-five kilograms of surplus honey the first year."

"This is preposterous!" Mr. Jerome exploded, his highly trained sensitivities deeply offended.

"Experienced beekeepers figure one to two hectares of heavy flowering plants for each colony of bees," the old man went on. "Of course, in my small rooming house it was out of the question. Then I saw this beautiful land and acquired property of my own."

"It's dreadful—unheard of," Jerome sputtered.

"You don't need much capital," the old man continued with enthusiasm. "Only queen-size cells with eggs inside and some royal jelly. The worker bees do the rest."

"All this time, a veritable factory." Mr. Jerome was beside himself. "All right under my very nose."

"With good beekeeping management, the colonies should increase to thirty in a few years."

"Oh, no!" Jerome's well-modulated voice rose to a shout: "Look here, I won't have it. You must stop this at once!"

"Why should you want me to stop?"

"For obvious reasons: we can't have the mourners stung..."

"Mr. Jerome, I have done you a great service. Your flowers have never been so magnificent or plentiful."

"That's true," he was forced to admit.

"Why? Because of my bees. They pollinate your flowers. Now, if you could spare me a few moments."

At that particular second Mr. Jerome was fully occupied, easing another attacker gently off the lapel of his serge suit. All his spare time would be devoted to a solution of Mr. Blake's special problem. *It must be illegal*, he thought, with every intention of rushing back to the office to examine the small print.

The old man straightened and looked at him proudly.

"Mr. Jerome, I have reached an important decision: I should like to buy another lot."

———

Are Mr. Jerome's objections valid? Why or why not?

Could this story have a sequel? What might happen next?

If you were to develop a radio, television, or magazine ad for Mr. Blake's new business, what would you say?

Maelstrom II

BY ARTHUR C
CLARKE

He flashed a quick glance at Earth, Moon, and receding spacecraft, and made his decision. The safety line whipped away as he snapped the quick release; now he was alone, a half a million kilometres from Earth.

He was not the first man, Cliff Leyland told himself bitterly, to know the exact second and the precise manner of his death; times beyond number, condemned criminals had waited for their last dawn. Yet until the very end, they could have hoped for a reprieve; human judges can show mercy, but against the laws of nature there was no appeal.

And only six hours ago he had been whistling happily while he packed his ten kilos of personal baggage for the long fall home.

He could still remember (even now, after all that had happened) how he had dreamed that Myra was already in his arms, that he was taking Brian and Sue on that promised cruise down the Nile. In a few minutes, as Earth rose above the horizon, he might see the Nile again; but memory alone could bring back the faces of his wife and children. And all because he had tried to save nine hundred and fifty sterling dollars by riding home on the freight catapult instead of the rocket shuttle.

He had expected the first twelve seconds of the trip to be rough, as the electric launcher whipped the capsule along its fifteen-kilometre track and shot him off the Moon. Even with the protection of the water bath in which he had floated during countdown, he had not looked forward to the twenty g of takeoff. Yet when the acceleration had gripped the capsule, he had been hardly aware of the immense forces acting upon him. The only sound was a faint creaking from the metal walls; to anyone who had experienced the thunder of a rocket launch, the silence was uncanny. When the cabin speaker had announced, "T plus five seconds—speed three thousand kilometres an hour," he could scarcely believe it.

Three thousand kilometres an hour from a standing start—with seven seconds still to go as the generators smashed their thunderbolts of power into the launcher. He was riding the lightning across the face of the Moon; and at T plus seven seconds, the lightning failed.

Even in the womb-like shelter of the tank, Cliff could sense that something had gone wrong. The water around him, until now frozen almost rigid by its weight, seemed suddenly to become alive. Though the capsule was still hurtling along the track, all acceleration had ceased and it was merely coasting under its own momentum.

He had no time to feel fear, or to wonder what had happened, for the power failure lasted little more than a second. Then, with a jolt that shook the capsule from end to end and set off a series of ominous, tinkling crashes, the field came on again.

When the acceleration faded for the last time, all weight vanished with it. Cliff needed no instrument but his stomach to tell that the capsule had left the end of the track and was rising away from the surface of the Moon. He waited impatiently until the automatic pumps had drained the tank and the hot-air driers had done their work; then he drifted across the control panel and pulled himself down into the bucket seat.

"Launch Control," he called urgently, as he drew the restraining straps around his waist. "What the devil happened?"

A brisk but worried voice answered at once.

"We're still checking—call you back in thirty seconds. Glad you're okay," it added belatedly.

While he was waiting, Cliff switched to forward vision. There was nothing ahead except stars—which was as it should be. At least he had taken off with most of his planned speed and there was no danger that he would crash back to the Moon's surface immediately. But he would crash back sooner or later, for he could not possibly have reached escape velocity. He must be rising out into space along a great ellipse—and, in a few hours, he would be back at his starting point.

"Hello, Cliff," said Launch Control suddenly. "We've found what happened. The circuit breakers tripped when you went through section five of the track, so your take-off speed was just over a thousand kilometres an hour low. That will bring you back in just over five hours—but don't worry; your course-correction jets can boost you into a stable orbit. We'll tell you when to fire them; then all you have to do is sit tight until we can send someone to haul you down."

Slowly, Cliff allowed himself to relax. He had forgotten the capsule's vernier rockets; low-powered though they were, they could kick him into an orbit that would clear the Moon. Though he might fall back to within a few kilometres of the lunar surface, skimming over mountains and plains at a breath-taking speed, he would be perfectly safe.

Then he remembered those tinkling crashes from the control compartment, and his hopes dimmed again—for there were not many things that could break in a space vehicle without most unpleasant consequences.

He was facing those consequences, now that the final checks of the ignition circuits had been completed. Neither on manual nor on auto would the navigation rockets fire; the capsule's modest fuel reserves, which could have taken him to safety, were utterly useless. In five hours, he would complete his orbit—and return to his launching point.

I wonder if they'll name the new crater after me? thought Cliff. "Crater Leyland—diameter..." What diameter? Better not exaggerate—I don't suppose it will be more than two hundred metres across. Hardly worth putting on the map.

Launch Control was still silent, but that was not surprising; there was little that one could say to a man already as good as dead. And yet, though he knew that nothing could alter his trajectory, even now he did not believe that he would soon be scattered over most of Farside. He was still soaring away from the Moon, snug and comfortable in his little cabin. The idea of death was utterly incongruous—as it is to all men until the final second.

And then, for a moment, Cliff forgot his own problem. The horizon ahead was no longer flat; something even more brilliant than the blazing lunar landscape was lifting against the stars. As the capsule curved round the edge of the Moon, it was creating the only kind of Earthrise that was possible—a man-made one. In a minute it was all over, such was his speed in orbit. By that time the Earth had leaped clear of the horizon and was climbing swiftly up the sky.

It was three-quarters full and almost too bright too look upon. Here was a cosmic mirror made not of dull rocks and dusty plains, but of snow and cloud and sea. Indeed, it was almost all sea, for the Pacific was turned toward him, and the blinding reflection of the Sun covered the Hawaiian Islands. The haze of the atmosphere—that soft blanket that should have cushioned his descent in a few hours' time—obliterated all geographical details; perhaps that darker patch emerging from night was New Guinea, but he could not be sure.

There was a bitter irony in the knowledge that he was heading straight toward that lovely, gleaming apparition. Another thousand kilometres an hour—that was all. He might as well ask for a million.

The sight of the rising Earth brought home to him, with irresistible force, the duty he feared but could postpone no longer.

"Launch Control," he said, holding his voice steady with a great effort. "Please give me a circuit to Earth."

This was one of the strangest things he had ever done in his life—sitting here above the Moon, listening to the telephone ring in his own home a half a million kilometres away. It must be near midnight down there in Africa and it would be some time before there would be any answer. Myra would stir sleepily—then, because she was a spaceman's wife, always alert for disaster, she would be instantly awake. But they had both hated to have a phone in the bedroom, and it would be at least fifteen seconds before she could switch on the lights, close the nursery door to avoid disturbing the baby, get down the stairs and—

Her voice came clear and sweet across the emptiness of space. He would recognize it anywhere in the universe, and he detected at once the undertone of anxiety.

"Mrs. Leyland?" said the Earthside operator. "I have a call from your husband. Please remember the two-second time lag."

Cliff wondered how many people were listening to this call, either on the Moon, the Earth, or the relay satellites. It was hard to talk for the last time to your loved ones, not knowing how many eavesdroppers there might be. But as soon as he began to speak, no one else existed but Myra and himself.

"Darling," he began. "This is Cliff. I'm afraid I won't be coming home as promised. There's been a—a technical slip. I'm quite all right at the moment, but I'm in big trouble."

He swallowed, trying to overcome the dryness in his mouth, then went on quickly before she could interrupt. As briefly as he could, he explained the situation. For his own sake as well as hers, he did not abandon all hope.

"Everyone's doing their best," he said. "Maybe they can get a ship up to me in time—but in case they can't—well, I wanted to speak to you and the children."

She took it well, as he had known she would. He felt pride as well as love when her answer came back from the dark side of Earth.

"Don't worry, Cliff. I'm sure they'll get you out and we'll have our holiday after all, exactly the way we planned."

"I think so, too," he lied. "But just in case—would you wake the children? Don't tell them that anything's wrong."

It was an endless half minute before he heard their sleepy yet excited voices. Cliff would willingly have given these last few hours of his life to see their faces once again, but the capsule was not equipped with such luxuries as phonevision. Perhaps it was just as well, for he could not have hidden the truth had he looked into their eyes. They would know it soon enough, but not from him. He wanted to give them only happiness in these last moments together.

Yet it was hard to answer their questions, to tell them that he would soon be seeing them, to make promises that he could not keep. It needed all of his self-control when Brian reminded him of the Moon dust he had forgotten once before—but had remembered this time.

"I've got it, Brian—it's in a jar right beside me—soon you'll be able to show it to your friends." (No: Soon it will be back on the world from which it came.) "And Susie—be a good girl and do everything that Mummy tells you. Your last school report wasn't too good, you know, especially those remarks about behaviour…Yes, Brian, I have those photographs, and the piece of rock from Aristarchus—"

It was hard to die at thirty-five; but it was hard, too, for a boy to lose his father at ten. How would Brian remember him in the years ahead? Perhaps as no more than a fading voice from space, for he had spent so little time on Earth. In these last few minutes, as he swung outward and then back to the Moon, there was little enough that he could do except project his love and his hope across the emptiness that he would never span again. The rest was up to Myra.

When the children had gone, happy but puzzled, there was work to do. Now was the time to keep one's head, to be businesslike and practical. Myra must face the future without him, but at least he could make the transition easier. Whatever happens to the individual, life goes on; and modern life involves mortgages and instalments, insurance policies and joint bank accounts. Almost impersonally, as if they concerned someone else—which would soon be true enough—Cliff began to talk about these things. There was a time for the heart and a time for the brain. The heart would have its final say three hours from now, when he began his last approach to the surface of the Moon.

No one interrupted them; there must have been silent monitors maintaining the link between two worlds, but they might have been the only people alive. Sometimes, while he was speaking, Cliff's eyes would stray to the periscope and be dazzled by the glare of Earth—now more than halfway up the sky. It was impossible to believe that it was home for seven billion souls. Only three mattered to him now.

It should have been four, but with the best will in the world he could not put the baby on the same footing as the others. He had never seen his younger son; and now he never would.

At last, he could think of no more to say. For some things, a lifetime was not enough—but an hour could be too much. He felt physically and emotionally exhausted, and the strain on Myra must have been equally great. He wanted to be alone with his thoughts and with the stars, to compose his mind and to make his peace with the Universe.

"I'd like to sign off for an hour or so, darling," he said. There was no need for explanations; they understood each other too well. "I'll call you back in—in plenty of time. Goodbye for now."

He waited the two seconds for the answering goodbye from Earth; then cut the circuit and stared blankly at the tiny control desk. Quite unexpectedly, without desire or volition, tears sprang into his eyes, and suddenly he was weeping like a child.

He wept for his loved ones and for himself. He wept for the future that might have been and the hopes that would soon be incandescent vapour, drifting between the stars. And he wept because there was nothing else to do.

After a while he felt much better. Indeed, he realized that he was extremely hungry; there was no point in dying on an empty stomach, and he began to rummage among the space rations in the closet-sized galley. While he was squeezing a tube of chicken-and-ham paste into his mouth, Launch Control called.

There was a new voice at the end of the line—a slow, steady and immensely competent voice that sounded as if it would brook no nonsense from inanimate machinery.

"This is Van Kessel, Chief of Maintenance, Space Vehicles Division. Listen carefully, Leyland—we think we've found a way out. It's a long shot—but it's the only chance you have."

Alternations of hope and despair are hard on the nervous system. Cliff felt a sudden dizziness; he might have fallen, had there been any direction in which to fall.

"Go ahead," he said faintly, when he had recovered. Then he listened to Van Kessel with an eagerness that slowly changed to incredulity.

"I don't believe it!" he said at last. "It just doesn't make sense!"

"You can't argue with the computers," answered Van Kessel. "They've checked the figures about twenty different ways. And it makes sense all right; you won't be moving as fast at apogee, and it doesn't need much of a kick then to change your orbit. I suppose you've never been in a deep-space rig before?"

"No, of course not."

"Pity—but never mind. If you follow instructions you can't go wrong. You'll find the suit in the locker at the end of the cabin. Break the seals and haul it out."

Cliff floated the full two metres from the control desk to the rear of the cabin, and pulled on the lever marked: EMERGENCY ONLY—TYPE 17 DEEP-SPACE SUIT. The door opened and the shining silver fabric hung flaccid before him.

"Strip down to your underclothes and wriggle into it," said Van Kessel. "Don't bother about the biopack—you clamp that on later."

"I'm in," said Cliff presently. "What do I do now?"

"You wait twenty minutes—and then we'll give you the signal to open the air lock and jump."

The implications of the word "jump" suddenly penetrated. Cliff looked around the now familiar, comforting little cabin, and then thought of the lonely emptiness between the stars—the unreverberant abyss through which a man could fall until the end of time.

He had never been in free space; there was no reason why he should. He was just a farmer's boy with a master's degree in agronomy, seconded from the Sahara Reclamation Project and trying to grow crops on the Moon. Space was not for him; he belonged to the worlds of soil and rock, of Moon dust and vacuum-formed pumice.

"I can't do it," he whispered. "Isn't there any other way?"

"There's not," snapped Van Kessel. "We're doing our damnedest to save you, and this is no time to be neurotic. Dozens of men have been in far worse situations—badly injured, trapped in wreckage a million kilometres from help. But you're not even scratched, and already you're squealing! Pull yourself together—or we'll sign off and leave you to stew in your own juice."

Cliff turned slowly red, and it was several seconds before he answered.

"I'm all right," he said at last. "Let's go through those instructions again."

"That's better," said Van Kessel approvingly. "Twenty minutes from now, when you're at apogee, you'll go into the air lock. From that point, we'll lose communication: Your suit radio has only a fifteen-kilometre range. But we'll be tracking you on radar and we'll be able to speak to you when you pass over us again. Now, about the controls on your suit..."

The twenty minutes went quickly enough; at the end of that time, Cliff knew exactly what he had to do. He had even come to believe that it might work.

"Time to bail out," said Van Kessel. "The capsule's correctly oriented—the air lock points the way you want to go. But direction isn't critical—*speed* is what matters. Put everything you've got into that jump—and good luck!"

"Thanks," said Cliff inadequately. "Sorry that I—"

"Forget it," interrupted Van Kessel. "Now get moving!"

For the last time, Cliff looked round the tiny cabin, wondering if there was anything that he had forgotten. All his personal belongings would have to be abandoned, but they could be replaced easily enough. Then he remembered the little jar of Moon dust he had promised Brian; this time, he would not let the boy down. The minute mass of the sample—only a few grams—would make no difference to his fate; he tied a piece of string round the neck of the jar and attached it to the harness of his suit.

The air lock was so small that there was literally no room to move; he stood sandwiched between inner and outer doors until the automatic pumping sequence was finished. Then the wall slowly opened away from him and he was facing the stars.

With his clumsy, gloved fingers, he hauled himself out of the air lock and stood upright on the steeply curving hull, bracing himself tightly against it with the safety line. The splendour of the scene held him almost paralyzed; he forgot all his fears of vertigo and insecurity as he gazed around him, no longer constrained by the narrow field of vision of the periscope.

The Moon was a gigantic crescent, the dividing line between night and day a jagged arc sweeping across a quarter of the sky. Down there the sun was setting, at the beginning of the long lunar night, but the summits of isolated peaks were still blazing with the last light of day, defying the darkness that had already encircled them.

That darkness was not complete. Though the Sun was gone from the

land below, the almost full Earth flooded it with glory. Cliff could see, faint but clear in the glimmering Earthlight, the outlines of seas and highlands, the dim stars of mountain peaks, the dark circles of craters. He was flying above a ghostly, sleeping land—a land which was trying to drag him to his death. For now he was poised at the highest point of his orbit, exactly on the line between Moon and Earth. It was time to go.

He bent his legs, crouching against the hull. Then, with all his force, he launched himself toward the stars, letting the safety line run out behind him.

The capsule receded with surprising speed, and as it did so, he felt a most unexpected sensation. He had anticipated terror or vertigo—but not this unmistakable, haunting sense of familiarity. All this had happened before; not to him, of course, but to someone else. He could not pinpoint the memory, and there was no time to hunt for it now.

He flashed a quick glance at Earth, Moon, and receding spacecraft, and made his decision without conscious thought. The safety line whipped away as he snapped the quick release; now he was alone, three thousand kilometres above the Moon, a half a million kilometres from Earth. He could do nothing but wait; it would be two and a half hours before he would know if he could live—and if his own muscles had performed the task that the rockets had failed to do.

And then, as the stars slowly revolved around him, he suddenly knew the origin of that haunting memory. It had been many years since he had read Poe's short stories; but who could ever forget them?

He, too, was trapped in a maelstrom, being whirled down to his doom; he too, hoped to escape by abandoning his vessel. Though the forces involved were totally different, the parallel was striking. Poe's fisherman had lashed himself to a barrel because stubby, cylindrical objects were being sucked down into the great whirlpool more slowly than his ship. It was a brilliant application of the laws of hydrodynamics; Cliff could only hope that his use of celestial mechanics would be equally inspired.

How fast had he jumped away from the capsule? At a good eight kilometres per hour, surely. Trivial though that speed was by astronomical standards, it should be enough to inject him into a new orbit—one that, Van Kessel had promised him, would clear the Moon by several kilometres. That was not much of a margin, but it would be enough on this airless world, where there was no atmosphere to draw him down.

With a sudden spasm of guilt, Cliff realized that he had never made that second call to Myra. It was Van Kessel's fault; the engineer had kept him on the move, given him no time to brood over his own affairs. And Van Kessel was right: In a situation like this, Cliff could think only of himself. All his resources, mental and physical, must be concentrated on survival. This was no time or place for the distracting and weakening ties of love.

He was racing now toward the night side of the Moon, and the daylit crescent was shrinking even as he watched. The intolerable disk of the Sun, toward which he dared not look, was falling swiftly toward the curved horizon. The crescent moonscape dwindled to a burning line of light, a bow of fire set against the stars. Then the bow fragmented into a dozen shining beads, which one by one winked out as he shot into the shadow of the Moon.

With the going of the Sun, the Earthlight seemed more brilliant than ever, frosting his suit with silver as he rotated slowly along his orbit. It took him about ten seconds to make each revolution; there was nothing he could do to check his spin, and indeed he welcomed the constantly changing view. Now that his eyes were no longer distracted by occasional glimpses of the Sun, he could see the stars in thousands where there had been only hundreds before. The familiar constellations were drowned, and even the brightest of the planets were hard to find in that blaze of light.

The dark disk of the lunar nightland lay across the star field like an eclipsing shadow, and it was slowly growing as he fell toward it. At every instant some star, bright or faint, would pass behind its edge and wink out of existence. It was almost as if a hole were growing in space, eating up the heavens.

There was no other indication of his movement, or of the passage of time—except for his regular ten-second spin. When Cliff looked at his watch, he was astonished to see that he had left the capsule half an hour ago. He searched for it among the stars, without success. By now, it would be several kilometres behind—but presently it would draw ahead of him, as it moved on its lower orbit, and would be the first to reach the Moon.

Cliff was still puzzling over this paradox when the strain of the last few hours, combined with the euphoria of weightlessness, produced a result he would have hardly believed possible. Lulled by the gentle susurration of the air inlets, floating lighter than any feather as he turned beneath the stars, he fell into a dreamless sleep.

When he awoke at some prompting of his subconscious, the Earth was nearing the edge of the Moon. The sight almost brought on another wave of self-pity, and for a moment he had to fight for control of his emotions. This was the very last he might ever see of Earth, as his orbit took him back over Farside, into the land where the Earthlight never shone. The brilliant Antarctic ice caps, the equatorial cloud belts, the scintillation of the Sun upon the Pacific—all were sinking swiftly behind the lunar mountains. Then they were gone; he had neither Sun nor Earth to light him now, and the invisible land below was so black that it hurt his eyes.

Unbelievably, a cluster of stars had appeared *inside* the darkened disk, where no stars could possibly be. Cliff stared at them in astonishment for a few seconds, then realized he was passing above one of the Farside settlements. Down there beneath the pressure domes of their city, people were waiting out the lunar night—sleeping, working, loving, resting, quarreling...Did they know that he was speeding like an invisible meteor through their sky, racing above their heads at over six thousand kilometres an hour? Almost certainly, for by now the whole Moon, and the whole Earth, must know of his predicament. Perhaps they were searching for him with radar and telescope, but they would have little time to find him. Within seconds, the unknown city had dropped out of sight, and he was once more alone above Farside.

It was impossible to judge his altitude above the blank emptiness speeding below, for there was no sense of scale or perspective. But he knew that he was still descending, and that at any moment one of the crater walls or mountain peaks that strained invisibly toward him might claw him from the sky.

For in the darkness somewhere ahead was the final obstacle—the hazard he feared most of all. Across the heart of Farside; spanning the equator from north to south in a wall almost two thousand kilometres long, lay the Soviet Range. He had been a boy when it was discovered, back in 1959, and could still remember his excitement when he had seen the first smudged photographs from Lunik III. He could never have dreamed that one day he would be flying toward those same mountains, waiting for them to decide his fate.

The first eruption of dawn took him completely by surprise. Light exploded ahead of him, leaping from peak to peak until the whole arc of the horizon was limned with flame. He was hurtling out of the lunar night, directly into the face of the Sun. At least he would not die in darkness, but the greatest danger was yet to come. For now he was almost back where he had started, nearing the lowest point of his orbit. He glanced at the suit chronometer, and saw that five full hours had now passed. Within minutes, he would have hit the Moon—or skimmed it and passed safely out into space.

As far as he could judge, he was less than forty kilometres above the surface, and he was still descending, though very slowly now. Beneath him, the long shadows of the lunar dawn were daggers of darkness stabbing into the nightland. The steeply slanting sunlight exaggerated every rise in the ground, making even the smallest hills appear to be mountains. And now, unmistakably, the land ahead was rising, wrinkling into the foothills of the Soviet Range. More than a hundred and fifty kilometres away, but approaching at over a kilometre a second, a wave of rock was climbing from the face of the Moon. There was nothing he could do to avoid it; his path was fixed and unalterable. All that could be done had already been done, two and a half hours ago.

It was not enough. He was not going to rise above these mountains; they were rising above him.

Now he regretted his failure to make that second call to the woman who was still waiting, a half a million kilometres away. Yet perhaps it was just as well, for there had been nothing more to say.

Other voices were calling in the space around him, as he came once more within range of Launch Control. They waxed and waned as he flashed through the radio shadow of the mountains; they were talking about him, but the fact scarcely registered on his emotions. He listened with an impersonal interest, as if to messages from some remote point of space or time, of no concern to him. Once he heard Van Kessel's voice say, quite distinctly: "Tell *Callisto's* skipper we'll give him an intercept orbit, as soon as we know that Leyland's past perigee. Rendezvous time should be one hour, five minutes from now." I hate to disappoint you, thought Cliff, but that's one appointment I'll never keep.

For now the wall of rock was only seventy-five kilometres away, and each time he spun helplessly in space it came fifteen kilometres closer. There was no room for optimism now, as he sped more swiftly than a rifle bullet toward that implacable barrier. This was the end, and suddenly it became of great importance to know whether he would meet it face first, with open eyes, or with his back turned, like a coward.

No memories of his past life flashed through Cliff's mind as he counted the seconds that remained. The swiftly unrolling moonscape rotated beneath him, every detail sharp and clear in the harsh light of dawn. Now he was turned away from the onrushing mountains, looking back on the path he had travelled, the path that should have led to Earth. No more than three of his ten-second days were left to him.

And then the moonscape exploded into silent flame. A light as fierce as that of the Sun banished the long shadows, struck fire from the peaks and craters spread below. It lasted for only a fraction of a second, and had faded completely before he had turned toward its source.

Directly ahead of him, only thirty kilometres away, a vast cloud of dust was expanding toward the stars. It was as if a volcano had erupted in the Soviet Range—but that, of course, was impossible. Equally absurd was Cliff's second thought—that by some fantastic feat of organization and logistics the Farside Engineering Division had blasted away the obstacle in his path.

For it was gone. A huge, crescent-shaped bite had been taken out of the approaching skyline; rocks and debris were still rising from a crater that had not existed five seconds ago. Only the energy of an atomic bomb, exploded at precisely the right moment in his path, could have wrought such a miracle. And Cliff did not believe in miracles.

He had made another complete revolution and was almost upon the mountains when he remembered that all this while there had been a cosmic bulldozer moving invisibly ahead of him. The kinetic energy of the abandoned capsule—a thousand tonnes, traveling at over a kilometre a second—was quite sufficient to have blasted the gap through which he was now racing. The impact of the man-made meteor must have jolted the whole of Farside.

His luck held to the very end. There was a brief pitter-patter of dust particles against his suit, and he caught a blurred glimpse of glowing rocks and swiftly dispersing smoke clouds flashing beneath him. (How strange to see a cloud upon the Moon!) Then he was through the mountains, with nothing ahead but blessed, empty sky.

Somewhere up there, an hour in the future along his second orbit, *Callisto* would be moving to meet him. But there was no hurry now; he had escaped from the maelstrom. For better or for worse, he had been granted the gift of life.

There was the launching track, a few kilometres to the right of his path; it looked like a hairline scribed across the face of the Moon. In a few moments he would be within radio range; now, with thankfulness and joy, he could make that second call to Earth, to the woman who was still waiting in the African night.

———

What did you expect after reading the first paragraph? Were your expectations fulfilled?

What parts made you anxious? Sad? Hopeful? Relieved? Happy?

Arthur C. Clarke has long been a popular science-fiction writer. Why do you think this is so, judging from the story?

Uneasy Home-coming

BY WILL F. JENKINS

The window was broken. A neat jagged section of glass was missing. It had been cracked and removed so that someone could reach in and unlock it.

onnie began to have the feeling of dread and uneasiness in the taxi but told herself it was not reasonable. She dismissed it decisively when she reached the part of town in which all her friends lived. She could stop and spend the evening with someone until Tom got home, but she didn't. She thrust away the feeling as the taxi rolled out across the neck of land beyond most of the houses. The red, dying sun cast long shadows across the road.

So far, their house was the only one that had been built on the other side of the bay. But she could see plenty of other houses as the taxi drew up before the door. Those other houses were across the bay, to be sure, but there was no reason to be upset. She was firm with herself.

The taxi stopped and the last thin sliver of crimson sun went down below the world's edge. Dusk was already here. But everything looked perfectly normal. The house looked neat and hospitable, and it was good to be back. She paid the taxi driver and he obligingly put her suitcases inside the door. The uneasy feeling intensified as he left. But she tried not to heed it.

It continued while she heard the taxi moving away and purring down the road. But it remained essentially the same—a formless restlessness and apprehension—until she went into the kitchen. Then the feeling changed.

She was in the kitchen, with the close smell of a shut-up house about her, when she noticed the change. Her suitcases still lay in the hall where the taxi driver had piled them. The front door was still open to let in fresh air. And quite suddenly, she had an urgent conviction that there was something here that she should notice. Something quite inconspicuous. But this sensation was just as absurd as the feeling she'd had in the taxi.

There was a great silence outside the house. This was dusk, and bird and insect noises were growing fainter. There were no neighbours near to make other sounds.

She turned on the refrigerator, and it began to make a companionable humming sound. She turned on the water, and it gushed. But there her queer sensation took a new form. It seemed that every movement pro- duced a noise which advertised her presence, and she felt that there was some reason to be utterly still. And that really was nonsense too.

She glanced into the dining room. She regarded her luggage still piled in the hall near the open front door. Everything looked exactly as every- thing should look when one returns from a two weeks' holiday and one's husband has been away on business at the same time. Tom would get home about midnight. She had spoken to him on the telephone yesterday. He would positively get back in a few hours. So it would be absurd not to stay here to greet him. The feeling she had, she decided firmly, was simply a normal dislike of being alone. And she would not be silly.

She glanced around the kitchen. Afterwards she remembered that she had looked straight at the back door without seeing what there was to be seen. She went firmly down the hall. Then she went out of doors to look at her flowers.

The garden looked only a little neglected. The west was a fading, already dim glory of red and gold. She could not see too many details, but the garden was fragrant and appealing in the dusk. She saw the garage— locked and empty, of course, since Tom had the car—and felt a minor urge to go over to it. But she did not. Afterwards the memory of that minor urge made her feel faint. But it was only an idea. She dismissed it.

She smelled the comfortable, weary smells of the late summer evening, which would presently give way to the sharper, fresher scents of night. There was the tiny darting shadow of a bat overhead, black against the dark sapphire sky. It was the time when, for a little space, peace seems to enfold all the world. But the nagging uneasiness persisted even out here.

There was a movement by the garage, but it failed to catch her eye. If she had looked—even if she failed to see the movement—she might still have seen the motorcycle. It did not belong here, but it was leaning against the garage wall as if its owner had ridden it here and leaned it confidentially where it would be hidden from anyone looking across the bay. But Connie noticed nothing. She simply felt uneasy.

She found herself going nervously back towards the house. The sunset colours faded, and presently all would be darkness outside. She heard her footsteps on the gravelled walk. Occasional dry leaves brushed against her feet. It seemed to her that she hurried, which was ridiculous. So she forced herself to walk naturally and resisted an impulse to look about.

That was why she failed to notice the pantry window.

She came to the front of the house. Her heels made clicking sounds on the steps. She felt a need to be very quiet, to hide herself.

Yet she had no reason for fear in anything she actually had noticed. She hadn't seen anything odd about the back door or the pantry window, and she hadn't noticed the motorcycle or the movement by the garage. The logical explanation for her feeling of terror was simply that it was dark and she was alone.

She repeated that explanation as she forced herself to enter the dark front doorway.

She wanted to gasp with relief as she felt for the switch and the lights came on. The dark rooms remaining were more terrifying then than the night outside. So she went all over the ground floor, turning on lights, and tried not to think of going upstairs. There was no one within call and no one but the taxi driver even knew that she was here. Anything could happen.

But she did not know anything to cause danger either.

Connie had felt and fought occasional fear before. To bring her nameless frights into the light for scorn, she had talked lightly in the past of the imaginary Things towards which people feel such terror—and Things which nervous people believe are following them; the Things imagined to be hiding in cupboards and behind dark trees in deserted streets. But her past scorn failed to dispel her terror now. She tried to be angry with herself because she was being as silly as a neurotic person who cannot sleep without first taking a look under the bed at night. But still, Connie could not drive herself to go upstairs or to look under her own bed right now.

It was an unfortunate omission.

In the lighted living room she had the feeling of someone staring at her from the dark outside. It was unbearable. She went to the telephone, absolutely certain that there was nothing wrong. But if she talked to someone—

She called Mrs. Winston. It was not a perfect choice. Mrs. Winston was not nearly of Connie's own age, but Connie felt so sorry for the older woman that when she needed comfort she often instinctively called her. Talking to someone else who needed comforting always seemed to make one's own troubles go away.

Mrs. Winston's voice was bright and cheery over the phone. "My dear Connie! How nice it is that you're back with us!"

Connie felt better instantly. She felt herself relaxing, she heard her voice explaining that she'd had a lovely holiday and that Tom was coming back tonight and—

Mrs. Winston said anxiously, "I do hope your house is all right, Connie. Is it? It's been dreadful here! Did you hear?"

"Not a word since I left," said Connie. "What's happened?"

She expected to hear about someone having been unkind to Charles, who was Mrs. Winston's only son. He gave Connie the creeps, but she could feel very sorry for his mother. He had a talent for getting into trouble. There'd been a girl when he was only sixteen, he had been caught stealing in school when there was no excuse for it, and he'd been expelled from college and nowadays wore an apologetic air. Mrs. Winston tried to believe that he was simply having a difficult time growing up. But he was already twenty, and at twenty a hulking young man with an apologetic air and a look of always thinking of something else—one could sympathize with his mother and still feel uncomfortable about him.

Mrs. Winston's voice went on explaining. And the feeling of terror came back upon Connie like a blow.

There had been a series of burglaries in the town. The Hamiltons' house had been ransacked while they were out for an evening's bridge. The Blairs' house was looted while they were away. The Smithsons'. The

Tourneys'. And Saddler's shop was robbed, and the burglars seemed to know exactly where Mr. Saddler kept his day's receipts and took them and the tray of watches and fountain pens and the cameras. And poor Mr. Field—

Mr. Field was the ancient cashier at Saddler's. He had interrupted the burglars, and they had beaten him horribly, leaving him for dead. He had never regained consciousness, and it was not believed now at the hospital that he ever would.

Connie said from a dry throat, "I wish you hadn't told me that tonight. I'm all alone. Tom won't be back until midnight."

"But my dear," Mrs. Winston exclaimed, "you mustn't. I'll locate Charles and have him come for you right away! You can spend the evening here, and he can take you back when—"

Connie shook her head at the telephone. "Oh, no! That would be silly!"

She heard her voice refusing, and her mind protested the refusal. But Charles made her flesh crawl. She could not bear to think of him driving her through the darkness. Baseless terror was bad enough, she thought, without actual aversion besides.

"I'm quite all right!" she insisted. "Quite! I do hope Mr. Field gets better, but I'm all right..."

When she hung up the phone she was aware that she was sick. But it was startling to discover that her knees were physically weak when she started to move from the instrument. She could telephone someone else, and they would come for her. But Mrs. Winston would be offended and take it as an affront. And Connie was still sure that her fear was quite meaningless. It was just a feeling.

She moved aimlessly away from the telephone, found herself at the foot of the stairs. Then she looked up at the dark above and wanted to whimper. But a saving fury came to her. She would not yield to groundless fear. She was in terror of—she called it burglars now, but it actually it was of Them, the unknown men women are taught to fear as dangerous.

"Ridiculous!" Connie told herself.

She got a suitcase and started for the stairs. It was deep night now. If she looked out—say, at the garage—she would see nothing. Somewhere there was a dismal cooing. Doves.

She climbed the stairs into darkness. Nothing happened. She pressed a switch and the passage sprang into light. She breathed again. She went into Tom's and her bedroom. There was dust on the dressing table. There was an ashtray. She put down the suitcase and was conscious of bravery because she was angry.

Then she saw cigarette butts on the rug. Scorched places. Someone had sat in this bedroom, smoking and indifferently dropping cigarette butts on the rug and crushing them out.

Connie stood with every muscle in her body turned to stone.

A part of Connie's brain directed her eyes again to the bed. Someone had sat on it—only sat—and smoked at leisure. But a corner of the bedspread was twitched aside. What was under the bed? She found herself backing away from it, into a chair which toppled over. The noise made her freeze.

But nothing happened. There was no change in the companionable hum of the refrigerator downstairs. No reaction to the sound of the overturned chair—which seemed incredible. If one of Them—the nameless Things of which she was in terror now—was under the bed, he would come out at the noise.

Presently—her breathing loud in her own ears—Connie bent and looked under the bed. She had to. None of Them was under it. Of course. But there was object there which was strange.

A very long time later, Connie dragged it out. It was a bag with bulges in it. Her hands shook horribly, but she dumped its contents on the floor. There were cameras. Silver. Sally Hamilton's necklace and rings. There were watches and fountain pens. This must be what the burglars had taken from the Hamiltons' house and the Blairs' and the Smithsons' and the Tourneys'. The cameras and pens and watches came from Saddler's shop, where Mr. Field had come upon the burglars and they had beaten him almost to death. The burglars had nearly killed him.

Connie went to the bedroom door. Her knees were water. Her house had been used as the hiding place for the loot of the burglaries that had taken place in her absence. But now if they found out she was back—

Without much rationalization, she could guess why Mr. Field had been nearly killed. He must have recognized the burglars. And now they could look across the bay and see that Connie was home. Wouldn't they know instantly that she would soon find their loot? And that she then would telephone for the police...?

Unless they came and stopped her. Quickly.

Shivering, Connie turned out the light in her bedroom. And in the upstairs hall. Downstairs, she turned out the light in the living room, went quickly to the front door and bolted it. She was leaving it when she thought to fumble her way across the room and make sure that the window was locked. It was. If the lights had been seen across the bay.... She hastened desperately to turn out the rest. The dining room. Lights out. The windows were locked. The pantry. It was dark. Whimpering, she was afraid to enter it. She flashed on the light to make sure of the window.

The window was broken. A neat jagged section of glass was missing. It had been cracked and removed so that someone could reach in and unlock it. It was now impossible to lock; anyone could reach in and unfasten it again.

Connie snapped off the light and fled into the kitchen and made that dark. But as the bulb dimmed she realized what she had seen in the very act of snapping the light switch. The back door was not fully closed. Its key was missing. There was mud on the floor where someone had come in—more than once. The burglars must have made casual, constant use of the house.

She stood panting in the blackness. Somewhere outside, frogs croaked. There was a thump, and her heart stood still until she realized that a night-flying insect had bumped against the window.

The refrigerator cut off.

It was coincidence, of course, but it was shocking. The proper thing, the logical thing, was to go to the telephone now. She could not see to dial, but somehow she must.

She felt her way blindly to the instrument. Her fingers on the wall made whispering sounds that guided her and she became aware of the loud pounding sound her heart made.

Just as she reached the telephone there was a faint noise which might have been a footstep in the garden.

She waited, filled with such fear that her body did not seem to exist and she had no physical sensation at all.

But a part of her brain saw with infinite despair that if the burglars had been near the house at sunset, intending to enter it as soon as darkness fell, they would have seen the taxi deliver her. They would have known sooner or later she would discover proof of their presence. And what she had just done told them of her discovery! The light in the bedroom where their loot was hidden turned out.... Every other light turned out. They would know she had darkened the house to hide in it, to use the telephone.

There was a soft sound at the back door. It squeaked.

Connie stood rigid. The clicking of the dial would tell everything. She could not conceivably summon help.

There was the soft whisper of a foot on the kitchen linoleum. Connie's hands closed convulsively. The one thought that came to her now was she must breathe quietly.

There was a grey glow somewhere. The figure in the kitchen was throwing a flashlight beam on the floor. Then it halted, waiting. He knew that she was hiding somewhere in the house.

He went almost soundlessly into the living room. She saw the glow of the light there. Back into the kitchen. She heard him moving quietly—listening—towards the door through which she had come only a few seconds before to use the telephone.

He came through that door, within a metre of her. But when he was fully through the doorway she was behind him. Again he flashed the light downwards. But he did not think to look behind him. By just so much she was saved for the moment.

In the greyish light reflected from the floor she recognized him.

He went into the dining room. He moved very quietly, but he bumped ever so slightly against a chair. The noise made her want to shriek. He was hunting her, and he knew that she was in the house and he had to kill her. He had to get his loot and get away, and she must not be able to tell anything about him.

He was back in the kitchen again. He stood there, listening, and Connie was aware of a new and added emotion which came of her recognition of him. She felt that she would lie down at any instant and scream—because she knew him!

He came towards the door again, but he went up the stairs. They creaked under his weight. He must have reasoned cunningly that she would want to hide, because she was afraid. So he would go into the bedroom and look under the bed....

Connie slipped her feet out of her slippers. He had not reached the top of the stairs before she stood in her stockinged feet in the blackness below.

The front door was impossible. She would have to unlock it, make a noise. But he had not closed the back door behind him.

She crept out of it, with a passionate care that almost vanished when she was in the blessed night. There were stars. She remembered that she must not step on the gravel on which her feet might make a noise, so she stepped on the grass. And she fled.

There were sounds inside the house. He was opening cupboards, deliberately making sounds to fill her with panic as he hunted her down. He hadn't guessed yet that she was outside.

There were shrubs by the garage, so she slowed her flight to avoid them. And then she came upon the motorcycle. She smelled it, oil and gasoline and rubber. It was useless to her. She had no idea how to operate it. But suddenly a wild escape occurred to her—the motorcycle wasn't entirely useless.

Connie fumbled with the machine in the dark. She turned a tap. The smell of gasoline grew strong. There was a crash inside the house. But outside, the night was full of stars, and the air was cool and sweet—except that the smell of gasoline was growing stronger in it.

Connie had a book of matches in her pocket. Quickly she got it out, and in one motion struck a match and dropped it and ran away into the darkness, with the strange feel of grass under her feet.

The gasoline blazed fiercely. She hid herself in the shadows and watched, sobs trying to form in her throat. The fire would be seen across the bay. It would plainly be at Connie's house. People would come quickly—a lot of them. And fire engines.

As the flames grew higher, she saw the figure plunge from the house, run furiously towards the fire, trying to flail it out. But it was impossible.

And he knew it. Even his twisted mind would tell him that nothing could hide his identity now. The motorcycle would be identification enough, and there was the loot in the house.

Connie found herself weeping. It was partly relief. But it was also the unnerving realization that the fears she'd had about Them, the men who prey on others, were not entirely groundless.

The headlights of cars began to focus towards the house, along the road from the mainland. The bells of fire engines started tolling and grew louder. And in the leaping flames surrounding the motorcycle, a hulking, desperate figure threw futile handfuls of earth upon the machine. Was he, Connie wondered, trying to create the hopeless pretence that he was the first to help?

Even so, she was quite safe now, Connie knew. She began to cry in reaction from her terror. But, also, she wept heartbrokenly for poor Mrs. Winston. She, Connie, could have been murdered. She could have been the victim of one of those twisted men who prey on their fellow beings. But she wept for Mrs. Winston.

She, Connie, would not now be one of the people They had killed. But Mrs. Winston was the mother of one of Them.

———

What else could Connie have done to deal with the intruder?

The author, Will F. Jenkins, decided to introduce suspense in the very first line. Was that a good decision? (You might try that in your own writing and see what happens.)

When exactly were you sure that there was an intruder in the house? What effect did that have on you as a reader?

The Way Up to Heaven

BY ROALD DAHL

"It's too late!" she cried to the chauffeur. "I can't wait for him, I simply can't. I'll miss the plane. Hurry now, driver, hurry! To the airport!"

All her life, Mrs. Foster had had an almost pathological fear of missing a train, a plane, a boat, or even a theatre curtain. In other respects, she was not a particularly nervous woman, but the mere thought of being late on occasions like these would throw her into such a state of nerves that she would begin to twitch. It was nothing much—just a tiny vellicating muscle in the corner of the left eye, like a secret wink—but the annoying thing was that it refused to disappear until an hour or so after the train or plane or whatever had been safely caught.

It is really extraordinary how in certain people a simple apprehension about a thing like catching a train can grow into a serious obsession. At least half an hour before it was time to leave the house for the station, Mrs. Foster would step out of the elevator all ready to go, with hat and coat and gloves, and then being quite unable to sit down, she would flutter and fidget about from room to room until her husband, who must have been well aware of her state, finally emerged from his privacy and suggested in a cool dry voice that perhaps they had better get going now, had they not?

Mr. Foster may possibly have had a right to be irritated by this foolishness of his wife's, but he could have had no excuse for increasing her misery by keeping her waiting unnecessarily. Mind you, it is by no means certain that this is what he did, yet whenever they were to go somewhere, his timing was so accurate—just a minute or two late, you understand—and his manner so bland that it was hard to believe he wasn't purposely inflicting a nasty private torture of his own on the unhappy lady. And one thing he must have known—that she would never dare to call out and tell him to hurry. He had disciplined her too well for that. He must also have known that if he was prepared to wait even beyond the last moment of safety, he could drive her nearly into hysterics. On one or two special occasions in the later years of their married life, it seemed almost as though he had *wanted* to miss the train simply in order to intensify the poor woman's suffering.

Assuming (though one cannot be sure) that the husband was guilty, what made his attitude doubly unreasonable was the fact that, with the exception of this one small irrepressible foible, Mrs. Foster was and always had been a good and loving wife for over thirty years. There was no doubt about this. Even she, a very modest woman, was aware of it, and although she had for years refused to let herself believe that Mr. Foster would ever consciously torment her, there had been times recently when she had caught herself beginning to wonder.

Mr. Eugene Foster, who was nearly seventy years old, lived with his wife in a large six-story house on East Sixty-second Street, and they had four servants. It was a gloomy place, and few people came to visit them. But on this particular morning in January, the house had come alive and there was a great deal of bustling about. One maid was distributing bundles of dust sheets to every room, while another was draping them over the furniture. The butler was bringing down suitcases and putting them in the hall. The cook kept popping up from the kitchen to have a word with the butler, and Mrs. Foster herself, in an old-fashioned fur coat and with a black hat on the top of her head, was flying from room to room and pretending to supervise these operations. Actually, she was thinking of nothing at all except that she was going to miss her plane if her husband didn't come out of his study soon and get ready.

"What time is it, Walker?" she said to the butler as she passed him.

"It's ten minutes past nine, Madam."

"And has the car come?"

"Yes, Madam, it's waiting. I'm just going to put the luggage in now."

"It takes an hour to get to Idlewild," she said. "My plane leaves at eleven. I have to be there half an hour beforehand for the formalities. I shall be late. I just *know* I'm going to be late."

"I think you have plenty of time, Madam," the butler said kindly. "I warned Mr. Foster that you must leave at nine fifteen. There's still another five minutes."

"Yes, Walker, I know, I know. But get the luggage in quickly, will you please?"

She began walking up and down the hall, and whenever the butler came by, she asked him the time. This, she kept telling herself, was the *one* plane she must not miss. It had taken months to persuade her husband to allow her to go. If she missed it, he might easily decide that she should cancel the whole thing. And the trouble was that he insisted on coming to the airport to see her off.

"Dear God," she said out loud, "I'm going to miss it. I know, I know, I *know* I'm going to miss it." The little muscle beside the left eye was twitching madly now. The eyes themselves were very close to tears.

"What time is it, Walker?"

"It's eighteen minutes past, Madam."

"Now I really *will* miss it!" she cried. "Oh, I wish he would come!"

This was an important journey for Mrs. Foster. She was going to Paris to visit her daughter, her only child, who was married to a Frenchman. Mrs. Foster didn't care much for the man, but she was fond of her daughter, and, more than that, she had developed a great yearning to set eyes on her three grandchildren. She knew them only from the many photographs that she had received and that she kept putting up all over the house. They were beautiful, these children. She doted on them, and each time a new picture arrived, she would carry it away and sit with it for a long time, staring at it lovingly and searching the small faces for signs of that old satisfying blood likeness that meant so much. And now, lately, she had come more and more to feel that she did not really want to live out her days in a place where she could not be near these children, and have them visit her, and take them for walks, and buy them presents, and watch them grow. She knew, of course, that it was wrong and in a way disloyal to have thoughts like these while her husband was still alive. She knew also that although he was no longer active in his many enterprises, he would never consent to leave New York and live in Paris. It was a miracle that he had ever agreed to let her fly over there alone for six weeks to visit them. But, oh, how she wished she could live there always, and be close to them!

"Walker, what time is it?"

"Twenty-two minutes past, Madam."

As he spoke, a door opened and Mr. Foster came into the hall. He stood for a moment, looking intently at his wife, and she looked back at him—at this diminutive but still quite dapper old man with the huge bearded face that bore such an astonishing resemblance to those old photographs of Andrew Carnegie.

"Well," he said, "I suppose perhaps we'd better get going fairly soon if you want to catch that plane."

"Yes, dear—yes! Everything's ready. The car's waiting."

"That's good," he said. With his head over to one side, he was watching her closely. He had a particular way of cocking the head and then moving it in a series of small, rapid jerks. Because of this and because he was clasping his hands up high in front of him, near the chest, he was somehow like a squirrel standing there—a quick clever old squirrel from the Park.

"Here's Walker with your coat, dear. Put it on."

"I'll be with you in a moment," he said. "I'm just going to wash my hands."

She waited for him, and the tall butler stood beside her, holding the coat and the hat.

"Walker, will I miss it?"

"No, Madam," the butler said. "I think you'll make it all right."

Then Mr. Foster appeared again, and the butler helped him on with his coat. Mrs. Foster hurried outside and got into the hired Cadillac. Her husband came after her, but he walked down the steps of the house slowly, pausing halfway to observe the sky and to sniff the cold morning air.

"It looks a bit foggy," he said as he sat down beside her in the car. "And it's always worse out there at the airport. I shouldn't be surprised if the flight's cancelled already."

"Don't say that, dear—please."

They didn't speak again until the car had crossed over the river to Long Island.

"I arranged everything with the servants," Mr. Foster said. "They're all going off today. I gave them half pay for six weeks and told Walker I'd send him a telegram when we wanted them back."

"Yes," she said. "He told me."

"I'll move into the club tonight. It'll be a nice change staying at the club."

"Yes, dear. I'll write to you."

"I'll call in at the house occasionally to see that everything's all right and to pick up the mail."

"But don't you really think Walker should stay there all the time to look after things?" she asked.

"Nonsense. It's quite unnecessary. And anyway, I'd have to pay him full wages."

"Oh yes," she said. "Of course."

"What's more, you never know what people get up to when they're left alone in a house," Mr. Foster announced, and with that he took out a cigar and, after snipping off the end with a silver cutter, lit it with a gold lighter.

She sat still in the car with her hands clasped together tight under the motor rug.

"Will you write to me?" she asked.

"I'll see," he said. "But I doubt it. You know I don't hold with letter-writing unless there's something specific to say."

"Yes, dear, I know. So don't you bother."

They drove on, along Queens Boulevard, and as they approached the flat marshland on which Idlewild is built, the fog began to thicken and the car had to slow down.

"Oh dear!" cried Mrs. Foster. "I'm *sure* I'm going to miss it now! What time is it?"

"Stop fussing," the old man said. "It doesn't matter anyway. It's bound to be cancelled now. They never fly in this sort of weather. I don't know why you bothered to come out."

She couldn't be sure, but it seemed to her there was suddenly a new note in his voice, and she turned to look at him. It was difficult to observe any change in his expression under all that hair. The mouth was what counted. She wished, as she had so often before, that she could see the mouth clearly. The eyes never showed anything except when he was in a rage.

"Of course," he went on, "if by any chance it *does* go, then I agree with you—you'll be certain to miss it now. Why don't you resign yourself to that?"

She turned away and peered through the window at the fog. It seemed to be getting thicker as they went along, and now she could only just make out the edge of the road and the margin of grassland beyond it. She knew that her husband was still looking at her. She glanced back at him again, and this time she noticed with a kind of horror that he was staring intently at the little place in the corner of her left eye where she could feel the muscle twitching.

"Won't you?" he said.

"Won't I what?"

"Be sure to miss it now if it goes. We can't drive fast in this muck."

He didn't speak to her any more after that. The car crawled on and on. The driver had a yellow light directed onto the edge of the road, and this helped him keep going. Other lights, some white and some yellow, kept coming out of the fog toward them, and there was an especially bright one that followed close behind them all the time.

Suddenly, the driver stopped the car.

"There!" Mr. Foster cried. "We're stuck. I knew it."

"No, sir," the driver said, turning round. "We made it. This is the airport."

Without a word, Mrs. Foster jumped out and hurried through the main entrance into the building. There was a mass of people inside, mostly disconsolate passengers standing around the ticket counters. She pushed her way through and spoke to the clerk.

"Yes," he said. "Your flight is temporarily postponed. But please don't go away. We're expecting the weather to clear any moment."

She went back to her husband who was still sitting in the car and told him the news. "But don't you wait, dear," she said. "There's no sense in that."

"I won't," he answered. "So long as the driver can get me back. Can you get me back, driver?"

"I think so," the man said.

"Is the luggage out?"

"Yes, sir."

"Goodbye, dear," Mrs. Foster said, leaning into the car and giving her husband a small kiss on the coarse grey fur of his cheek.

"Goodbye," he answered. "Have a good trip."

The car drove off, and Mrs. Foster was left alone.

The rest of the day was a sort of nightmare for her. She sat for hour after hour on a bench, as close to the airline counter as possible, and every thirty minutes or so she would get up and ask the clerk if the situation had changed. She always received the same reply—that she must continue to wait, because the fog might blow away at any moment. It wasn't until after six in the evening that the loudspeakers finally announced that the flight had been postponed until eleven o'clock the next morning.

Mrs. Foster didn't quite know what to do when she heard this news. She stayed sitting on her bench for at least another half-hour, wondering, in a tired, hazy sort of way, where she might go to spend the night. She hated to leave the airport. She didn't wish to see her husband. She was terrified that in one way or another he would eventually manage to prevent her from getting to France. She would have liked to remain just where she was, sitting on the bench the whole night through. That would be the safest. But she was already exhausted, and it didn't take her long to realize that this was a ridiculous thing for an elderly lady to do. So in the end she went to a phone and called the house.

Her husband, who was on the point of leaving for the club, answered it himself. She told him the news, and asked whether the servants were still there.

"They've all gone," he said.

"In that case, dear, I'll just get myself a room somewhere for the night. And don't you bother yourself about it at all."

"That would be foolish," he said. "You've got a large house here at your disposal. Use it."

"But, dear, it's *empty*."

"Then I'll stay with you myself."

"There's no food in the house. There's nothing."

"Then eat before you come in. Don't be so stupid. Everything you do, you seem to want to make a fuss about it."

"Yes," she said. "I'm sorry. I'll get myself a sandwich here, and then I'll come on in."

Outside, the fog had cleared a little, but it was still a long, slow drive in the taxi, and she didn't arrive back at the house on Sixty-second Street until fairly late.

Her husband emerged from his study when he heard her coming in. "Well," he said, standing by the study door, "how was Paris?"

"We leave at eleven in the morning," she answered. "It's definite."

"You mean if the fog clears."

"It's clearing now. There's a wind coming up."

"You look tired," he said. "You must have had an anxious day."

"It wasn't very comfortable. I think I'll go straight to bed."

"I've ordered a car for the morning," he said. "Nine o'clock."

"Oh, thank you, dear. And I certainly hope you're not going to bother to come all the way out again to see me off."

"No," he said slowly. "I don't think I will. But there's no reason why you shouldn't drop me at the club on your way."

She looked at him, and at that moment he seemed to be standing a long way off from her, beyond some borderline. He was suddenly so small and so far away that she couldn't be sure what he was doing, or what he was thinking, or even what he was.

"The club is downtown," she said. "It isn't on the way to the airport."

"But you'll have plenty of time, my dear. Don't you want to drop me at the club?"

"Oh, yes—of course."

"That's good. Then I'll see you in the morning at nine."

She went up to her bedroom on the third floor, and she was so exhausted from her day that she fell asleep soon after she lay down.

Next morning, Mrs. Foster was up early, and by eight thirty she was downstairs and ready to leave.

Shortly after nine, her husband appeared. "Did you make any coffee?" he asked.

"No, dear. I thought you'd get a nice breakfast at the club. The car is here. It's been waiting. I'm all ready to go."

They were standing in the hall—they always seemed to be meeting in the hall nowadays—she with her hat and coat and purse, he in a curiously cut Edwardian jacket with high lapels.

"Your luggage?"

"It's at the airport."

"Ah yes," he said. "Of course. And if you're going to take me to the club first, I suppose we'd better get going fairly soon, hadn't we?"

"Yes!" she cried. "Oh, yes—*please!*"

"I'm going to get a few cigars. I'll be right with you. You get in the car."

She turned and went out to where the chauffeur was standing, and he opened the car door for her as she approached.

"What time is it?" she asked him.

"About nine fifteen."

Mr. Foster came out five minutes later, and watching him as he walked slowly down the steps, she noticed that his legs were like goat's legs in those narrow stovepipe trousers that he wore. As on the day before, he paused halfway down to sniff the air and to examine the sky. The weather was still not quite clear, but there was a wisp of sun coming through the mist.

"Perhaps you'll be lucky this time," he said as he settled himself beside her in the car.

"Hurry, please," she said to the chauffeur. "Don't bother about the rug. I'll arrange the rug. Please get going. I'm late."

The man went back to his seat behind the wheel and started the engine.

"*Just* a moment!" Mr. Foster said suddenly. "Hold it a moment, chauffeur, will you?"

"What is it, dear?" She saw him searching the pockets of his overcoat.

"I had a little present I wanted you to take to Ellen," he said. "Now, where on earth is it? I'm sure I had it in my hands as I came down."

"I never saw you carrying anything. What sort of present?"

"A little box wrapped up in white paper. I forgot to give it to you yesterday. I don't want to forget it today."

"A little box!" Mrs. Foster cried. "I never saw any little box!" She began hunting frantically in the back of the car.

Her husband continued searching through the pockets of his coat. Then he unbuttoned the coat and felt around in his jacket. "Confound it," he said, "I must've left it in my bedroom. I won't be a moment."

"Oh, *please!*" she cried. "We haven't got the time! *Please* leave it! You can mail it. It's only one of those silly combs anyway. You're always giving her combs."

"And what's wrong with combs, may I ask?" he said, furious that she should have forgotten herself for once.

"Nothing, dear, I'm sure. But..."

"Stay here!" he commanded. "I'm going to get it."

"Be quick, dear! Oh, *please* be quick!"

She sat still, waiting and waiting.

"Chauffeur, what time is it?"

The man had a wristwatch, which he consulted. "I make it nearly nine thirty."

"Can we get to the airport in an hour?"

"Just about."

At this point, Mrs. Foster suddenly spotted a corner of something white wedged down in the crack of the seat on the side where her husband had been sitting. She reached over and pulled out a small paper-wrapped box, and at the same time she couldn't help noticing it was wedged down firm and deep, as though with the help of a pushing hand.

"Here it is!" she cried. "I've found it! Oh dear, and now he'll be up there forever searching for it! Chauffeur, quickly—run in and call him down, will you please?"

The chauffeur, a man with a small rebellious mouth, didn't care very much for any of this, but he climbed out of the car and went up the steps to the front door of the house. The he turned and came back. "Door's locked," he announced. "You got a key?"

"Yes—wait a minute."

She began hunting madly in her purse. The little face was screwed up tight with anxiety, the lips pushed outward like a spout.

"Here it is! No—I'll go myself. It'll be quicker. I know where he'll be."

She hurried out of the car and up the steps to the front door, holding the key in one hand. She slid the key into the keyhole and was about to turn it—and then she stopped. Her head came up, and she stood there absolutely motionless, her whole body arrested right in the middle of all this hurry to turn the key and get into the house, and she waited—five, six, seven, eight, nine, ten seconds, she waited. The way she was standing there, with her head in the air and the body so tense it seemed as though she were listening for the repetition of some sound that she had heard a moment before from a place far away inside the house.

Yes—quite obviously she was listening. Her whole attitude was a *listening* one. She appeared actually to be moving one of her ears closer and closer to the door. Now it was right up against the door, and for still another few seconds she remained in that position, head up, ear to the door, hand on key, about to enter but not entering, trying instead, or so it seemed, to hear and to analyze these sounds that were coming faintly from this place within the house.

Then, all at once, she sprang to life again. She withdrew the key from the door and came running back down the steps.

"It's too late!" she cried to the chauffeur. "I can't wait for him, I simply can't. I'll miss the plane. Hurry now, driver, hurry! To the airport!"

The chauffeur, had he been watching her closely, might have noticed that her face had turned absolutely white and that the whole expression had suddenly altered. There was no longer that rather soft and silly look. A peculiar hardness had settled itself upon the features. The little mouth, usually so flabby, was now tight and thin, the eyes were bright, and the voice, when she spoke, carried a new note of authority.

"Hurry, driver, hurry!"

"Isn't your husband travelling with you?" the man asked, astonished.

"Certainly not! I was only going to drop him at the club. It won't matter. He'll understand. He'll get a cab. Don't sit there talking, man. *Get going!* I've got a plane to catch to Paris!"

With Mrs. Foster urging him from the back seat, the man drove fast all the way, and she caught the plane with a few minutes to spare. Soon she was high up over the Atlantic, reclining comfortably in her airplane chair, listening to the hum of the motors, heading for Paris at last. The new mood was still with her. She felt remarkably strong and, in a queer sort of way, wonderful. She was a trifle breathless with it all, but this was more from pure astonishment at what she had done than anything else, and as the plane flew farther and farther away from New York and East Sixty-second Street, a great sense of calmness began to settle upon her. By the time she reached Paris, she was just as strong and cool and calm as she could wish.

She met her grandchildren, and they were even more beautiful in the flesh than in their photographs. They were like angels, she told herself, so beautiful they were. And every day she took them for walks and fed them cakes, and bought them presents, and told them charming stories.

Once a week, on Tuesdays, she wrote a letter to her husband—a nice, chatty letter—full of news and gossip, which always ended with the words "Now be sure to take your meals regularly, dear, although this is something I'm afraid you may not be doing when I'm not with you."

When the six weeks were up, everybody was sad that she had to return to America, to her husband. Everybody, that is, except her. Surprisingly, she didn't seem to mind as much as one might have expected, and when she kissed them all goodbye, there was something in her manner and in the things she said that appeared to hint at the possibility of a return in the not too distant future.

However, like the faithful wife she was, she did not overstay her time. Exactly six weeks after she had arrived, she sent a telegram to her husband and caught the plane back to New York.

Arriving at Idlewild, Mrs. Foster was interested to observe that there was no car to meet her. It is possible that she might even have been a little amused. But she was extremely calm and did not overtip the porter who helped her into a taxi with her baggage.

New York was colder than Paris, and there were lumps of dirty snow lying in the gutters of the streets. The taxi drew up before the house on Sixty-second Street, and Mrs. Foster persuaded the driver to carry her two large suitcases to the top of the steps. Then she paid him off and rang the bell. She waited, but there was no answer. Just to make sure, she rang again, and she could hear it tinkling shrilly far away in the pantry, at the back of the house. But still no one came.

She took out her own key and opened the door herself.

The first thing she saw when she entered was a great pile of mail lying on the floor where it had fallen after being slipped through the letter hole. The place was dark and cold. A dust sheet was still draped over the grandfather clock. In spite of the cold, the atmosphere was peculiarly oppressive, and there was a faint but curious odor in the air that she had never smelled before.

She walked quickly across the hall and disappeared for a moment around the corner to the left, at the back. There was something deliberate and purposeful about this action; she had the air of a woman who is off to investigate a rumour or to confirm a suspicion. And when she returned a few seconds later, there was a little glimmer of satisfaction on her face.

She paused in the centre of the hall, as though wondering what to do next. Then, suddenly, she turned and went across into her husband's study. On the desk she found his address book, and after hunting through it for a while she picked up the phone and dialled a number.

"Hello," she said. "Listen—this is Nine East Sixty-second Street. . . . Yes, that's right. Could you send someone round as soon as possible, do you think? Yes, it seems to be stuck between the second and third floors. At least, that's where the indicator's pointing. . . . Right away? Oh, that's very kind of you. You see, my legs aren't any too good for walking up a lot of stairs. Thank you so much. Goodbye."

She replaced the receiver and sat there at her husband's desk, patiently waiting for the man who would be coming soon to repair the elevator.

———

Did you suspect something would happen to Mr. Foster? How did the author, Roald Dahl, cause you to suspect it?

How do you feel about this kind of "retributive justice"?

The Opened Order

BY ILSE AICHINGER

He felt the envelope in his pocket and fingered the seal. In the failing light the itch to open it mounted like a fever within him.

No instructions had come from headquarters for a long time, and it looked as if they were going to stay there for the winter. In the fields all around the last berries were falling from the bushes and rotting in the moss. Sentries sat forlornly in the tree-tops and watched the falling shadows. The enemy lay beyond the river and did not attack. Instead the shadows grew longer every evening, and every morning the mist clung more stubbornly to the hollows. Among the young volunteers of the defending army there were some who resented this kind of warfare, and they had made up their minds to attack, if need be without orders, before the snow came.

When therefore one of them was ordered one morning to take a message to headquarters, he had an uncomfortable feeling of foreboding. Careless though they seemed in other matters, he knew that they would stand no nonsense in the event of mutiny. Some questions that were put to him after he had delivered his message almost reminded him of an interrogation, and increased his uneasiness.

He found it all the more surprising therefore when, after a long wait, he was given an order in a sealed envelope, with instructions to get back to his unit before nightfall.

He was told to take the shorter way, which was shown him on the map, and, to his displeasure, a man was detailed to go with him. Through the open window he could see the beginning of the road he had to take. After crossing the clearing it disappeared wantonly between the hazel bushes. He was warned again to take extreme care, and then set off.

It was soon after midday. Clouds drifted across the sun and grazing cattle wandered over the grass and vanished unconcernedly into the thickets. The road was bad, and in places almost impassable because of encroachment by undergrowth. As soon as the driver put on a little speed, branches started hitting them in the face. The forest seemed to be waiting for the wood gatherers, and the river down below, when they caught glimpses of it from time to time through a clearing, seemed totally unconcerned. On the crests felled timber gleamed in the midday sun. Nothing in nature showed any awareness of the proximity of a frontier.

Every now and again they emerged from between the tree-trunks into open fields, which gave them a better view, and also enabled a better view to be had of them; they crossed them as quickly as possible. The driver bounced the vehicle over the roots of trees, and every now and then glanced back at the man with the order, as if to make sure that his load was all right. This made him angry, and convinced him of his superiors' mistrust.

What had his message contained? He had heard that early that morning one of the distant posts had observed movement on the other side of the river, but such rumours were continually in circulation, and it was possible that they were invented by the staff to keep the troops quiet. But it was equally possible that sending him to deliver the message had been a subterfuge, and that the confidence shown in him was sheer dissimulation. If his message had contained something unexpected, it would emerge from the contents of the order that he was taking back. He said to himself that it would be better to find out what it said now, while they were travelling in an area under enemy observation. When he was asked why he had broken the seal he could give some explanation on these lines. He felt the envelope in his pocket and fingered the seal. In the failing light the itch to open it mounted like a fever within him.

To gain time he asked the driver to change places with him. Driving calmed him. They had been driving through the woods for hours. In places the track was covered with rubble where obstacles had been built, and from this it was evident that they were nearing their destination. This proximity filled the man with indifference; perhaps it would prevent him from breaking the seal. He drove on calmly and confidently. At a spot where the track suddenly curved and plunged downwards in a suicidal manner they escaped without harm, but immediately afterwards the vehicle came to a halt in the middle of a mud patch. The engine had failed, and the cries of the birds made the quiet deeper than ever. Ferns grew all around. They dragged the vehicle out of the mud. The driver set about finding out the cause of the trouble. While he was lying underneath the vehicle the man hesitated no further, but broke open the envelope, scarcely bothering even to preserve the seal. He leant over the vehicle and read the order, which said that he was to be shot!

He managed to put it back in his breast-pocket before the driver scrambled out and announced that everything was now in order. He asked whether he should drive on. Yes, he should. While he bent over the starting-handle the man wondered whether to shoot him now or while he was driving. He had no doubt now that his driver was an escort.

The track broadened out, as if it repented of its sudden plunge downwards, and started gently mounting. "The soul of a suicide, carried by angels," the man quoted to himself. But the angles had been taking a soul to judgment, and the supposedly innocent act had turned out to be a guilty one. It had been action without orders. What surprised him was the trouble that was being taken with him.

In the falling darkness he could make out the other man's outline in front of him, the silhouette of his head and shoulders—an unquestioningness of outline that was denied to him. The sharp outlines of consciousness dissolve in the dark.

The driver turned and said: "We shall have a quiet night." This sounded like the sheerest irony. But their closeness to their destination seemed to make him talkative, and he went on, without waiting for an answer: "That is, if we get there safely!" The man took his revolver from its holster. It was so dark in the wood that one might have supposed that night had already fallen. "When I was a boy," the driver said, "I used to have to walk home from school through the woods. When it was dark I always used to sing!"

They reached the last clearing unexpectedly quickly. He decided to kill the driver as soon as they had crossed it, because there the wood grew thick again, before it opened out on reaching the burned-out hamlet where his unit lay. But this clearing was bigger than the others, and the river gleamed from a closer distance. A web of moonlight lay over the fields, which stretched all the way to the crest. The track was rutted by the wheels of ox-carts. In the moonlight the dry ruts looked like the inside of a death-mask; to anyone looking down across the clearing towards the river the earth bore the impression of an alien face.

The man rested his revolver on his knees. When the first shot rang out he had the impression that he had fired prematurely, against his will. But if his companion had been hit, his ghost must have had great presence of mind, because it accelerated and and drove on. It took a relatively long time to discover that it was not the driver, but he himself who had been hit. His arm sagged, and he dropped his revolver. More shots rang out before they reached the cover of the wood again, but they all missed.

The ghost in front turned his cheerful face towards him. "We were lucky to get across," he said. "That field was under observation." "Stop!" the man exclaimed. "Not here," the driver answered, "we had better go a little deeper into the wood." "I've been hit," the man said in desperation. The driver drove on a little way without looking round, and then stopped. He managed to staunch the flow of blood and tie up the wound. Then he said the only comforting thing he could think of. "We're nearly there," he said. A wounded man condemned to death, the man said to himself. "Wait!" he said aloud. "Is anything else the matter?" the driver said impatiently. "The order," the man said, and felt in his breast-pocket. At the moment of his deepest despair he had read its contents in a new light. The order said the bearer was to be shot, but mentioned no names.

"Take it," he said. "My coat is covered in blood." If his companion refused to take it, it would put the matter beyond doubt. After a moment's silence he felt the envelope being taken from his hand. "All right," said the driver.

The last half-hour passed in silence. Time and distance had turned into wolves devouring each other. Sheep are protected in the heavenly pastures, but the latter turned out to be a place of execution.

The unit was quartered in a hamlet of five farmhouses, of which three had been burned out in earlier skirmishes. The ease with which they could make out the undamaged houses made it clear that the virginity of the evening had not yet yielded to night. The place was surrounded by forest, the grass had been trampled down, and vehicles and guns were standing about. Barbed wire marked off the area from the surrounding forest.

When the sentry asked him his business, the driver said he had a wounded man with him, and had brought an order. They drove round the area. While the wounded man tried to sit up he thought to himself that this place was no more of a goal than any other place in the wide world. They were all to be regarded as points of departure rather than of arrival. He heard a voice asking: "Is he conscious?" and kept his eyes shut. It was important to gain time.

He had found new strength and new weapons to facilitate his flight before anything else happened. When they lifted him out of the vehicle he hung limply in their arms.

They carried him into one of the houses across a yard in the middle of which was a well. Two dogs snuffed about him. The wound hurt. They laid him on a bench in a room on the ground floor. The windows were open, and there was no light. "You look after him," the driver said. "I mustn't lose any more time."

The man expected them to come and dress his wound, but when he cautiously opened his eyes he found himself alone. Perhaps they had gone to fetch the first aid kit. There was a lively coming and going in the house, the sound of voices and footsteps and doors being slammed. But all this contained its own peculiar hush and increased the surrounding silence, just as the shrieking of the birds had done. What is all this about? the man said to himself and, after a few more minutes in which no one appeared, he started considering the possibility of immediate flight. A number of rifles were in the room. He would tell the sentry he had been ordered back to headquarters with another message. He had the necessary papers. If he did so soon, nobody would know for certain.

He tried to sit up, but was surprised to find how great was the weakness which he thought he had been shamming. Impatiently he put his feet down and tried to get up, but found that he could not stand. He sat down again, and stubbornly tried a second time. In doing so he tore open the emergency dressing that the driver had put on his wound, and it started bleeding again. It opened with the vehemence of a hidden wish. He felt that blood seeping through his shirt and wetting the wood of the bench on which he had sunk back. Through the window he saw the sky over the white-washed farmhouse wall. He heard the noise of hooves; the horses were being put back in their stable. There was more activity in the house than ever; it grew noisier and noisier; something unexpected must have happened. He pulled himself up to the window, but collapsed again, and he called out, but no one heard. He had been forgotten.

As he lay there the revolt seething inside him yielded to a desperate cheerfulness. It struck him that bleeding to death was like escaping through a bolted door, by-passing all the sentries. The room, which was illuminated only by the reflection of the opposite wall as if by snowlight, revealed itself as circumstance; and was not solitude the purest kind of circumstance, and was not the flowing of blood action? As he had wished for action for its own sake, and not for the sake of his country's defence, the sentence that was being fulfilled on him was right. As he was sick of inaction on the frontier, it meant release.

Shots rang out in the distance. He opened his eyes and remembered. Handing the order to the driver had been stupid and useless. While he lay here bleeding to death, they were leading the man to execution among the débris of the burnt-out farmhouses. Perhaps they had already bound his eyes, and only his mouth was still half-open with surprise, and they were presenting, aiming, and...

When he came round he felt that his wound had been dressed. He thought it an unnecessary service carried out by the angels for a man who had bled to death, an act of mercy performed too late. "So we meet again!" he said to the driver, who was bending over him. Only when he noticed that an officer from the staff was standing at the foot of his bed did he realize with horror that he was not dead.

"The order!" he said. "What happened to the order?"

"It was damaged by the round that hit you," the officer answered, "but it was still legible."

"I should have delivered it myself," he said.

"We got here just in time," the driver interrupted. "The enemy has started a general assault."

"It was the news we were waiting for," the officer remarked as he turned to go. At the door he turned again and, just for the sake of saying something, added:

"It's just as well you didn't know the wording of the message. We had an extraordinary code-phrase for the beginning of the operation!"

Translated from the German by Eric Mosbacher

What would you have done if you were the young soldier?

In what way is this story a "twist on a twist"?

Imagine you are the editor of "Suspense Monthly," and you are thinking about including this story in your next issue. Would you ask the author to make any changes? What kind of changes?

OPPOSING FORCES

On The Bridge

BY TODD
STRASSER

*Before Seth could say anything, the husky
guy reached forward and lifted him off the
ground by the collar of his jacket. His feet
kicked in the air uselessly.*

"I beat up this guy at the
mall yesterday," Adam Lockwood
said. He was leaning on the stone
wall of the bridge, smoking a cigarette and watching the cars speed
by on the highway beneath him.
His black hair fell down into his
eyes.

"How come?" Seth Dawson
asked, leaning on the stone wall
next to him.

Adam shrugged. The turned-
up collar of his leather jacket rose
and fell along his neck. "He just
bugged me, that's all. He was bigger, probably a senior. I guess he

thought he could take me 'cause I was smaller. But I don't let anyone push me around."

"What'd you do to him?" Seth asked. He too was smoking a cigarette. It was his first ever, and he wasn't really inhaling. Just holding the smoke in his mouth for a while and then blowing it out.

"I'm pretty sure I broke his nose," Adam said. "I couldn't hang around to find out because the guy in the pizza place called the cops. I'm already in enough trouble with them."

"What for?" Seth asked. He noticed that when Adam took a drag, he seemed to hold the smoke in his mouth and then blow it out his nose. But it was probably just a different way of inhaling. Adam definitely inhaled.

"They just don't like me," Adam said. "You know how it is."

Seth nodded. Actually, he didn't know how it was. But there was no way he'd admit that. It was just pretty cool to think that the cops didn't like you. Seth was pretty sure the cops didn't even know who he was.

The two boys looked back down at the highway. It was a warm spring afternoon, and instead of taking the bus home after school, they'd decided to walk to the diner. There Adam had instructed Seth on how to feed quarters into the cigarette machine and get a pack of Marlboros. Seth had been really nervous about getting caught, but Adam told him it was no sweat. If the owner came out, you'd just tell him you were picking them up for your mother.

Now the pack of Marlboros was sticking out of the breast pocket of Seth's new denim jacket. It wasn't supposed to look new because he'd ripped the sleeves off and had washed it in the washing machine a hundred times to make it look old and worn. But somehow it had come out looking new and worn. Seth had decided to wear it anyway, but he felt like a fraud. Like a kid trying to imitate someone truly cool. On the other hand, Adam's leather jacket looked authentically old and worn. The right sleeve was ripped and the leather was creased and pliant. It looked like he'd been in a hundred fights with it. Seth had never been in a fight in his life. Not a serious punching fight, at least.

The other thing about Adam was, he wore the leather jacket to school every day. Adam wasn't one of these kids who kept their cool clothes in their lockers and only wore them in school because their parents wouldn't let them wear them at home. Seth had parents like that. His mother would have had a fit if she ever saw him wearing his sleeveless denim jacket, so he had to hide it in the garage every day before he went into the house. Then in the morning when he left for school he'd go through the garage and pick it up.

Seth leaned forward and felt the smooth cold granite of the bridge with his fingers. The bridge was old and made of large granite blocks. Its heavy stone abutments stood close to the cars that sped past on the highway beneath it. Newer bridges were made of steel. Their spans were longer and the abutments were farther from the road.

On the highway, a red Fiat convertible approached with two girls riding in the front seat. Adam waved, and one of the girls waved back. A second later the car shot under the bridge and disappeared. He turned to Seth and grinned. "Maybe they'll get off on the exit ramp and come back," he said.

"You think?" Seth asked. Actually, the thought made him nervous. "They must be old enough at least to drive."

"So?" Adam asked. "I go out with older girls all the time."

"Really?" Seth asked.

"Sure," Adam said. He took another drag off his cigarette and blew the smoke out of his nose. Seth wanted to try that, but he was afraid he'd start to cough or do something else equally uncool.

In the distance a big semitrailer appeared on the highway. Adam raised his arm in the air and pumped his fist up and down. The driver responded with three loud blasts of his air horns. A moment later the semi rumbled under them and disappeared.

"Let me try that," Seth said. Another truck was coming and he leaned over the stone ledge and jerked his arm up and down. But the trucker ignored him.

Adam laughed.

"How come it didn't work?" Seth asked.

"You gotta do it a special way," Adam told him.

"Show me," Seth said.

"Can't, man," Adam said. "You just have to have the right touch. It's something you're born with."

Seth smirked. It figured. It was just his luck to be born without the touch that made truckers blow their horns.

The traffic was gradually getting thicker as the afternoon rush hour approached. Many of the drivers and passengers in the cars seemed unaware of the two boys on the overpass. But a few others stared up through their windshields at them.

"Bet they're wondering if we're gonna drop something on them," Adam said. He lifted his hand in the air as if he was holding an imaginary rock. On the highway more of the people in the cars were watching now. Suddenly Adam threw his arm forward. Even though there was nothing in his hand, a woman driving a blue Toyota put her hands up in fear. Her car swerved momentarily out of its lane.

Seth felt his jaw drop. He couldn't believe Adam had done that. If the car had been going faster it might have gone out of control and crashed into the stone abutment next to the highway.

Meanwhile Adam grinned at him. "Scared her to death."

"Maybe we ought to go," Seth said, suddenly worried that they were going to get into trouble. What if a cop had seen them? Or what if the woman was really mad?

"Why?" Adam asked.

"She could get off and come back here."

Adam shrugged. "Let her," he said. "The last person in the world I'd be afraid of is some old lady." He took a drag off his cigarette and turned away to watch the cars again.

Seth kept glancing toward the exit ramp to see if the woman in the blue Toyota had gotten off. He was really tempted to leave, but he stayed because he liked being with Adam. It made him feel good that a cool guy like Adam let him hang around.

A few minutes passed and the blue Toyota still did not appear on the exit ramp. Seth relaxed a little. He had smoked his Marlboro almost all the way down to the filter and his mouth tasted awful. Smoke kept getting in his eyes and making them water. He dropped the cigarette to the sidewalk and crushed it under his sneaker, relieved to be finished with it.

"Here's the way to do it," Adam said. He took the butt of his cigarette between his thumb and middle finger and flicked it over the side of the bridge and down into the traffic. With a burst of red sparks it hit the windshield of a black Camaro passing below. Adam turned and grinned. Seth smiled back uncomfortably. He was beginning to wonder just how far Adam would go.

Neither of them saw the black Camaro pull off onto the exit ramp and come up behind them on the bridge. Seth didn't notice it until he heard a door slam. He turned and saw three big guys getting out of the car. They were all wearing nylon sweatsuits, and they looked strong. Seth suddenly decided that it was time to go, but he quickly realized that the three guys had spread out, cutting off any way to escape. He and Adam were surrounded.

"Uh, Adam." Seth nudged him with his elbow.

"Wha—?" Adam turned around and looked shocked. In the meantime the three big guys were coming closer. Seth and Adam backed against the bridge wall. Seth felt his stomach tighten. His heart began to beat like a machine gun. Adam looked pretty scared too. Was it Seth's imagination, or was his friend trembling?

"Which one of you twerps flicked that butt on my car?" The question came from the husky guy with a black moustache and long black hair that curled behind his ears.

Seth and Adam glanced at each other. Seth was determined not to tell. He didn't believe in squealing on his friends. But suddenly he noticed that all three guys were staring at him. He quickly looked at Adam and saw why. Adam was pointing at him.

Before Seth could say anything, the husky guy reached forward and lifted him off the ground by the collar of his jacket. His feet kicked in the air uselessly for a second and then he was thrown against the front fender of the Camaro. He hit with a thud and lost his breath. Before he had a chance to recover, the guy grabbed him by the hair and forced his face toward the windshield.

"Lick it off," he grumbled.

Seth didn't know what he was talking about. He tried to raise his head, but the husky guy pushed his face closer to the windshield. God, he was strong.

"I said, lick it."

Lick what? Seth wanted to shout. Then he looked down at the glass and saw the little spot of grey ash where Adam's cigarette had hit. Oh, no. He stiffened. The thought made him sick. He tried to twist his head around, but the guy leaned his weight against Seth and pushed his face down again.

"Till it's clean," the guy said, pressing Seth's face down until it was only a couple of centimetres from the smooth, tinted glass. Seth stared at the little spot of ash. With the husky guy's weight on him, he could hardly breathe. The car's fender was digging into his ribs. Where was Adam?

The husky guy leaned harder against him, squeezing Seth painfully against the car. He pushed Seth's face down until it actually pressed against the cool glass. Seth could feel a spasm in his chest as his lungs cried for air. But he clamped his mouth closed. He wasn't going to give the guy the satisfaction of seeing him lick that spot.

The husky guy must have known it. Suddenly he pulled Seth's head up, then slammed it back down against the windshield. *Wham!* Seth reeled backwards, his hands covering his nose and mouth. Everything felt numb, and he was certain his nose and some teeth were broken. He slipped and landed in a sitting position, bending forward, his throbbing face buried in his hands.

A second passed and he heard someone laugh. Looking up he saw the three guys get back into the Camaro. The car lurched away, leaving rubber.

"You're bleeding." Adam was standing over him. Seth took his hand away from his mouth and saw that it was covered with bright red blood. It was dripping down from his nose and chin onto his denim jacket, leaving red spots. At the same time he squeezed the bridge of his nose. It hurt, but somehow he knew it was not broken after all. He touched his front teeth with his tongue. They were all still there, and none felt loose.

"You want a hand?" Adam asked.

Seth nodded and Adam helped pull him up slowly. He was shaky on his feet and worried that his nose was going to start bleeding again. He looked down and saw that his denim jacket was covered with blood.

"I tried to help you," Adam said, "but one of them held a knife on me."

Seth glanced at him.

"It was a small knife," Adam said. "I guess he didn't want anyone to see it."

Seth felt his nose again. It was swollen and throbbed painfully. "Why'd you point at me?" he asked.

"I figured I could jump them if they made a move at you," Adam said. "How could I know they had knives?"

Seth shook his head. He didn't believe Adam. He started to walk toward home.

"You gonna make it okay?" Adam asked.

Seth nodded. He just wanted to be alone.

"I'll get those guys for you, man," Adam said. "I think I once saw one of them at the diner. I'm gonna go back there and see. Okay?"

Seth nodded again. He didn't even turn to watch Adam go.

On the way to his house, Seth stopped near some garbage cans a neighbour had put on the curb for collection. He looked down at his denim jacket. The spots of blood had turned dark. If he took it home and washed it now, the stains would probably make it look pretty cool. Like a jacket that had been worn in tonnes of fights. Seth smirked. He took it off and threw it in the garbage can.

———

If you had Adam for a friend, what would you want to tell him?

If you were Seth's friend, what would you say to him?

Do you think Adam learned anything from the incident on the bridge? How do you know?

The Moose and the Sparrow

BY HUGH GARNER

I knew that Moose was capable of going to almost any lengths to prevent Cecil leaving the camp without knuckling under at least once; his urge seemed to me to be almost insane.

From the very beginning Moose Maddon picked on him. The kid was bait for all of Maddon's cruel practical jokes around the camp. He was sent back to the toolhouse for left-handed saws, and down to the office to ask the pay cheater if the day's mail was in, though the rest of us knew it was only flown out every week.

The kid's name was Cecil, and Maddon used to mouth it with a simpering mockery, as if it pointed to the kid being something less than a man. I must admit that the name fitted him, for Cecil was the least likely lumberjack I've seen in over twenty-five years in lumber camps. Though we knew he was intelligent enough, and a man too, if smaller than most of us, we all kidded him, in the good-natured way a bunkhouse gang will. Madden however always lisped the kid's name as if it belonged to a woman.

Moose Maddon was as different from Cecil as it is possible for two human beings to be and still stay within the species. He was a big moose of a man, even for a lumber stiff, with a round unshaven face that looked down angrily and dourly at the world. Cecil on the other hand was hardly taller than an axe-handle, and almost as thin. He was about nineteen years old, with the looks of an inquisitive sparrow behind his thick horn-rimmed glasses. He had been sent out to the camp for the summer months by a distant relative who had a connection with the head office down in Vancouver.

That summer we were cutting big stuff in an almost inaccessible stand of Douglas fir about eighty kilometres out of Nanaimo. The logs were catted eight kilometres down to the river where they were bunked waiting for the drive. Cecil had signed on as a whistle punk, but after a few days of snarling the operation with wrong signals at the wrong time and threatening to hang the rigging-slingers in their own chokers, he was transferred to Maddon's gang as a general handyman. Besides going on all the ridiculous and fruitless errands for Moose, he carried the noon grub to the gangs from the panel truck that brought it out from camp, made the tea and took the saws and axes in to old Bobbins, the squint eye, to be sharpened.

For the first two weeks after he arrived, the jokes were the usual ones practised on a greenhorn, but when they seemed to be having little or no effect on his bumbling habits and even temper, Moose devised more cruel and intricate ones. One night Moose and a cohort of his called Lefevre carried the sleeping Cecil, mattress and all, down to the river and threw him in. The kid almost drowned, but when he had crawled up on shore and regained his breath he merely smiled at his tormenters and ran back to the bunkhouse, where he sat shivering in a blanket on the springs of his bunk till the sun came up.

Another time Moose painted a wide mustache with tar on Cecil's face while he slept. It took him nearly a week to get it all off, and his upper lip was red and sore-looking for longer than that.

Nearly all of us joined in the jokes on Cecil at first, putting a young raccoon in his bunk, kicking over his tea water, hiding his clothes or tying them in knots, all the usual things. It wasn't long though until the other men noticed that Moose Maddon's jokes seemed to have a grim purpose. You could almost say he was carrying out a personal vendetta against the kid for refusing to knuckle under or cry "Uncle." From then on everybody but Moose let the kid alone.

One evening a few of us sat outside the bunkhouse shooting the guff, Moose said, "Hey, Cecil dear, what do you do over on the mainland?"

"Go to school," Cecil answered.

Moose guffawed. "Go to school? At your age?"

Cecil just grinned.

"What school d'ya go to, Cecil? Kindergarten?" Moose asked him, guffawing some more.

"No."

"You afraid to tell us?"

"No."

"Well, what school d'ya go to?"

"U.B.C."

"What's that, a hairdressin' school?"

"No, the university."

"University! You!"

Moose, who was probably a Grade Four dropout himself, was flabbergasted. I'm sure that up until that minute he'd been living in awe of anybody with a college education.

"What you takin' up?" he asked, his face angry and serious now.

"Just an arts course," Cecil said.

"You mean paintin' pictures an' things?"

"No, not quite," the kid answered.

For once Moose had nothing further to say.

From then on things became pretty serious as far as Moose and Cecil were concerned. On at least two occasions the other men on the gang had to prevent Moose from beating the boy up, and old Bobbins even went so far as to ask Mr. Semple, the walking boss, to transfer the youngster to another gang. Since learning that Cecil was a college boy, Moose gave him no peace at all, making him do jobs that would have taxed the strength of any man in the camp, and cursing him out when he was unable to do them, or do them fast enough.

The kid may not have been an artist, as Moose had thought, but he could make beautiful things out of wire. Late in the evenings he would sit on his bunk and fashion belt-buckles, rings, and tie-clips from a spool of fine copper wire he'd found in the tool shed. He made things for several of the men, always refusing payment for them. He used to say it gave him something to do, since he couldn't afford to join in the poker games.

One evening late in the summer as I was walking along the river having an after-supper pipe, I stumbled upon Cecil curled up on a narrow sandy beach. His head was buried in his arms and his shoulders were heaving with sobs. I wanted to turn around without letting him know he'd been seen, but he looked so lonely crying there by himself that I walked over and tapped him on the shoulder.

He jumped as if I'd prodded him with a peavey, and swung around, his eyes nearly popping from his head with fright. The six weeks he'd spent working under Moose Maddon hadn't done his nerves any good.

"It's all right kid," I said.

"Oh! Oh, it's you, Mr. Anderson!"

He was the only person in the camp who ever called me anything but "Pop."

"I don't mean to butt in," I said. "I was just walking along here, and couldn't help seeing you. Are you in trouble?"

He wiped his eyes on his sleeve before answering me. Then he turned and stared out across the river.

"This is the first time I broke down," he said, wiping his glasses.

"Is it Moose?"

"Yes."

"What's he done to you now?"

"Nothing more than he's been doing to me all along. At first I took it—you know that, Mr. Anderson, don't you?"

I nodded.

"I thought that after I was out here a couple of weeks it would stop," he said. "I expected the jokes that were played on me at first. After all I was pretty green when I arrived here. When they got to know me the other men stopped, but not that—that Moose."

He seemed to have a hard time mouthing the other's name.

"When are you going back to school?" I asked him.

"In another couple of weeks."

"Do you think you can stand it until then?"

"I need all the money I can make, but it's going to be tough."

I sat down on the sand beside him and asked him to tell me about himself. For the next ten or fifteen minutes he poured out the story of his life; he was one of those kids who are kicked around from birth. His mother and father had split up while he was still a baby, and he'd been brought up in a series of foster homes. He'd been smart enough, though, to graduate from high school at seventeen. By a miracle of hard work and self-denial he'd managed to put himself through the first year of university, and his ambition was to continue on to law school. The money he earned from his summer work here at the camp was to go towards his next year's tuition.

When he finished we sat in silence for a while. Then he asked, "Tell me, Mr. Anderson, why does Maddon pick on me like he does?"

I thought about his question for a long time before answering it. Finally I said, "I guess that deep down Moose knows you are smarter than he is in a lot of ways. I guess he's—well, I guess you might say he's jealous of you."

"No matter what I do, or how hard I try to please him, it's no good."

"It never is," I said.

"How do you mean?"

I had to think even longer this time. "There are some men, like Moose Maddon, who are so twisted inside that they want to take it out on the world. They feel that most other men have had better breaks than they've had, and it rankles inside them. They try to get rid of this feeling by working it out on somebody who's even weaker than they are. Once they pick on you there's no way of stopping them short of getting out of their way or beating it out of their hide."

Cecil gave me a wry grin. "I'd never be able to beat it out of the—the Moose's hide."

"Then try to keep out of his way."

"I can't for another two weeks," he said. "I'm afraid that before then he'll have really hurt me."

I laughed to reassure him, but I was afraid of the same thing myself. I knew that Moose was capable of going to almost any lengths to prevent Cecil leaving the camp without knuckling under at least once; his urge seemed to me to be almost insane. I decided to talk to George Semple myself in the morning, and have the boy flown out on the next plane.

"I don't think Moose would go as far as to really hurt you," I said to him.

"Yes he would! He would, Mr. Anderson, I know it! I've seen the way he's changed. All he thinks about any more are ways to make me crawl. It's no longer a case of practical jokes; he wants to kill me!"

My reassuring laugh stuck in my throat this time. "In another two weeks, son, you'll be back in Vancouver, and all this will seem like a bad dream."

"He'll make sure I leave here crippled," Cecil said.

We walked back to the camp together, and I managed to calm him down some.

The next day I spoke to Semple, the walking boss, and convinced him we should get the boy out of there. There was never any thought of getting rid of Moose, of course. Saw bosses were worth their weight in gold, and the top brass were calling for more and more production all the time. Whatever else Moose was, he was the best production foreman in the camp. When Semple spoke to Cecil, however, the kid refused to leave. He said he'd made up his mind to stick it out until his time was up.

Though my gang was working on a different side than Maddon's, I tried to keep my eye on the boy from then on. For a week things went on pretty much as usual, then one suppertime Cecil came into the dining hall without his glasses. Somebody asked him what had happened, and he said there'd been an accident, and that Moose had stepped on them. We all knew how much of an accident it had been: luckily the kid had an old spare pair in his kit. Few of his gang had a good word for Moose any more, which only seemed to make him more determined to take his spite out on the kid.

That evening I watched Cecil fashioning a signet ring for one of the men out of wire and a piece of quartz the man had found. The way he braided the thin wire and shaped it around a length of thin sapling was an interesting thing to see. Moose was watching him too, but pretending not to. You could see he hated the idea of Cecil getting along so well with the other men.

"I was going to ask you to make me a new watch strap before you left," I said to Cecil. "But it looks like you're running out of wire."

The kid looked up. "I still have about seven and a half metres of it left," he said. "That'll be enough for what I have in mind. Don't worry, Mr. Anderson, I'll make the watch strap before I leave."

The next afternoon there was quite a bit of commotion over where Maddon's gang were cutting, but I had to wait until the whistle blew to find out what had happened. Cecil sat down to supper with his right hand heavily bandaged.

"What happened?" I asked one of Maddon's men.

"Moose burned the kid's hand," he told me. "He heated the end of a saw blade in the tea fire, and then called the kid to take it to the squint eye to be sharpened. He handed the hot end to Cecil, and it burned his hand pretty bad."

"But—didn't any of you?"

"None of us was around at the time. When we found out, big Chief went after Moose with a cant hook, but the rest of us held him back. He would have killed Moose. If Maddon doesn't leave the kid alone, one of us is going to have to cripple him for sure."

Moose had been lucky that The Chief, a giant Indian called Danny Corbett, hadn't caught him. I made up my mind to have Cecil flown out in the morning without fail, no matter how much he protested.

That evening the kid turned in early, and we made sure there was always one of us in the bunkhouse to keep him from being bothered by anybody. He refused to talk about the hand-burning incident at all, but turned his head to the wall when anybody tried to question him about it. Moose left shortly after supper to drink and play poker in Camp Three, a short hike away through the woods.

I woke up during the night to hear a man laughing near the edge of the camp, and Maddon's name being called. I figured it was Moose and Lefevre coming home drunk from Camp Three, where the bull cook bootlegged homebrew.

When I got up in the morning, Cecil was already awake and dressed, sitting on the edge of his bunk plaiting a long length of his copper wire, using his good hand and the ends of the fingers of the one that was burned.

"What are you doing up so early?" I asked him.

"I went to bed right after chow last night, so I couldn't sleep once it got light." He pointed to the plaited wire. "This is going to be your watch strap."

"But you didn't need to make it now, Cecil," I said. "Not with your hand bandaged and everything."

"It's all right, Mr. Anderson," he assured me. "I can manage it okay, and I want to get it done as soon as I can."

Just as the whistle blew after breakfast one of the jacks from Camp Three came running into the clearing shouting that Moose Maddon's body was lying at the bottom of a deep narrow ravine outside the camp. This ravine was crossed by means of a fallen log, and Moose must have lost his footing on it coming home drunk during the night. There was a free fall of more than twelve metres down to a rocky stream bed.

None of us were exactly broken-hearted about Moose kicking off that way, but the unexpectedness of it shocked us. We all ran to the spot, and the boys rigged a sling from draglines and hauled the body to the top of the ravine. I asked Lefevre if he'd been with Moose the night before, but he told me he hadn't gone over to Camp Three. Later in the day the district coroner flew out from Campell River or somewhere, and after inspecting the log bridge made us rig a handline along it. He made out a certificate of accidental death.

When they flew the body out, Cecil stood with the rest of us on the river bank, watching the plane take off. If I'd been in his place I'd probably have been cheering, but he showed no emotion at all, not relief, happiness, or anything else.

He worked on my watch strap that evening, and finished it the next day, fastening it to my watch and attaching my old buckle to it. It looked like a real professional job, but when I tried to pay him for it he waved the money aside.

It was another week before Cecil packed his things to leave. His hand had begun to heal up nicely, and he was already beginning to lose the nervous twitches he'd had while Moose was living. When he was rowed out to the company plane, all the boys from his bunkhouse were on the river bank to see him go. The last we saw of Cecil was his little sparrow smile, and his hand waving to us from the window.

One day in the fall I went out to the ravine to see how the handline was making it. It still shocked me to think that Maddon, who had been as sure-footed as a chipmunk, and our best man in a log-rolling contest, had fallen to his death the way he had. Only then did I notice something nobody had looked for before. In the bark of the trunks of two small trees that faced each other diagonally across the fallen log were burn marks that could have been made by wire loops. A length of thin wire rigged from one to the other would have crossed the makeshift footbridge just high enough to catch a running man on the shin, and throw him into the ravine. Maddon could have been running across the log that night, if he'd been goaded by laughter and taunts of somebody waiting at the other end. I remembered the sound of laughter and the shouting of Maddon's name.

I'm not saying that's what happened, you understand, and for all I know nobody was wandering around outside the bunkhouses on the night of Maddon's death, not Cecil or anybody else. Still, it gives me a queer feeling sometimes, even yet, to look down at my wrist. For all I know I may be the only man in the world wearing the evidence of a murder as a wristwatch strap.

———

How else do you think this conflict could have been settled?

Does this story, or any of the characters in it, remind you of others in the book? What are their similarities and differences?

How does this story show that things are not always what they seem to be?

A Man

B Y   E R N E S T   B U C K L E R

He should have known that the horse wanted to be left alone. But he kept at it. The horse laid back his ears.

—Call the man Joseph. Call his son Mark. Two scars had bracketed Mark's left eye since he was twelve. But they were periods, not brackets, in the punctuation of his life. The reason had to do with his father.

Joseph had none of the stiffness that goes with rock strength. He was one of those men who cast the broadest shadow, without there being any darkness in them at all. Yet there was always a curious awkwardness between him and his son. In a neighbour's house of a Sunday afternoon Mark might stand nearer to him than anyone else; but he never got onto his lap like the other kids got onto their fathers' laps. Joseph never teased him. He never made him any of those small-scale replicas of farm gear that the other men made their sons: tiny ox carts or trail sleds.

In any case, that kind of fussy workmanship was not his province. His instrument was the plow.

One day he came across Mark poking seeds between the potato plants.

"What's them?" he said.

Mark could dodge anyone else's questions; he could never answer his father with less than the whole truth.

"They're orange seeds," he said.

He'd saved them from the Christmas before. Oranges were such a seldom thing then that it was as if he was planting a mystery.

"They won't grow here," Joseph said.

Mark felt suddenly ridiculous, as he so often did when his father came upon anything fanciful he was doing: as if he had to shift himself to the sober footing of common sense. He dug the seeds out and planted them, secretly, behind the barn.

The night of the accident was one of those cold, drizzly nights in early summer when animals in the pasture huddle like forlorn statues. The sort of night when the cows never come.

School had ended that very day. This was the third year Mark had graded twice and he was very excited. All the time his mother washed the supper dishes he kept prattling on about the kings and queens of England he'd have in his studies next term. He felt so much taller than the "kid" he'd been yesterday.

His father took no part in the conversation, but he was not for that reason outside it—and everything Mark said was for his benefit too.

Joseph was waiting to milk. "Aint' it about time you got after the cows?" he said at last. He never ordered Mark. It would have caused the strangest sort of embarrassment if he ever had.

Cows! Mark winced. Right when he could almost *see* the boy Plantagenet robed in ermine and wearing the jewelled crown!

"They'll come, won't they?" he said. (He knew better.) "They come last night."

He never used good speech when his father was around. He'd have felt like a girl. (Though Joseph was a far wiser, far better educated man in the true sense than Mark would ever be.)

"They won't come a night like this," Joseph said. "They're likely holed up in a spruce thicket somewheres, outa the rain."

"I'll see if I can hear the bell," Mark said.

He went out on the porch steps and listened. There wasn't a sound.

"It's no use to wait for the bell," Joseph called. "They won't budge a hair tonight."

"Well, if they ain't got sense enough to come themselves a night like this," Mark said, as near as he'd ever come to sputtering at his father, "why can't they just stay out?"

"I'd never get em back to their milk for a week," Joseph said.

Mark went then, but, as Joseph couldn't help seeing, grudgingly.

He sat on the bars of the pasture gate and called. "*Co*-boss, *co*-boss..." But there wasn't the tinkle of a bell.

He loved to be out in a good honest rain, but this was different. He picked his steps down the pasture lane to avoid the clammy drops that showered from every bush or fern he touched.

He came to the first clearing, were Joseph had planted the burntland potatoes last year. The cows were nowhere to be seen. But Pedro, the horse, was there—hunched up and gloomy-looking in the drizzle. Mark couldn't bear to see him so downcast and not try to soothe him.

He went close and patted his rump. Pedro moved just far enough ahead to shake off his touch. It was the kind of night when the touch of anything sent a shivery feeling all through you.

He should have known that the horse wanted to be left alone. But he kept at it. He'd touch him, the horse would move ahead, he'd follow behind and touch him again. The horse laid back his ears.

And then, in a flash, Mark saw the big black haunch rear up and the hoof, like a sudden devouring jaw, right in front of his left eye. The horse wasn't shod or Mark would have been killed.

He was stunned. But in a minute he got to his feet again. He put his hand to his face. It came away all blood. He began to scream and run for home.

Joseph could hear him crying before he came in sight. He started to meet him. When Mark came through the alder thicket below the barn and Joseph saw he was holding his hand up to his face, he broke into a run. Before he got to the bars he could see the blood.

He didn't stop to let down a single bar. He leapt them. Mark had never seen him move like that in his life before. He grabbed Mark up and raced back to the house.

Within minutes the house was a hubbub of neighbours. Mark gloried in the breathless attention that everyone bent on him. He asked Joseph to hold him up to the mirror over the sink. "No, no, Joseph, don't..." his mother pleaded, but Joseph obeyed him. His face was a mass of cuts and bruises. He felt like a Plantagenet borne off the field with royal wounds.

Afterward, he remembered all the head-shakings: "That biggest cut there don't look too good to me. Pretty deep..."

And the offers of help: "I got some b'racit acit for washin out cuts, down home. I could git it in a minute..."

And the warnings: "No, *don't* let him lay down. Anyone's had a blow on the head, always keep em movin around..."

And he remembered his mother beseeching him over and over: "Can you see all right? Are you sure you can see all right?"

He didn't remember his father doing or saying anything flustered, unusual. But Joseph would be the one who'd quietly put the extra leaves in the dining-room table so they could lay him on it when the doctor came at last, to have the stitches taken. And when the doctor put him to sleep (though he confessed that this was risky, with Mark's weak heart) it would be Joseph's hand that held the chloroform cone without a tremor.

The doctor said that Mark must stay in bed for two whole weeks. Joseph came in to see him once each day and again just before bedtime. Mark's eye was now swollen shut and the color of thunder sunsets. Maybe he'd have the mirror in his hand, admiring his eye, when he heard his father coming. He'd thrust the mirror in under the bedclothes. They exchanged the same awkward sentences each time. Joseph was the sort of man who looks helplessly out of place in a bedroom. He never sat down.

The first morning Mark was allowed outdoors again he had planned to walk; but Joseph picked him up without a word and carried him.

He didn't protest. But this time there was no tumult of excitement as before to leave him mindless of his father's arms about him; now the unaccustomed feel of them seemed to make him aware of every gram of his own weight. And yet, though it was merely an ordinary fine summer's morning, it struck him as the freshest, greenest, sunniest he had ever seen.

The moment they left the house it was plain to him that this wasn't just an aimless jaunt. His father was taking him somewhere.

Joseph carried him straight across the house field and down the slope beyond—to where he'd stuck the orange seeds in the ground.

Mark saw what they were headed for before they got there. But he couldn't speak. If he had tried to, he'd have cried.

Joseph set him down beside a miniature garden.

Miniature, but with the rows as perfectly in line as washboard ribs. This had been no rough job for the plow. It had been the painstaking work of fork and spade and then the careful molding of his hands. He must have started it right after the accident, because the seeds were already through the ground. And he hadn't mentioned it to a soul.

"This can be yours," he said to Mark.

"Oh, Father," Mark began, "it's..." But how could he tell him what it was? He bent down to examine the sprouts. "What's them?" he said, touching the strange plants in the outside row.

"Melons," Joseph said, pointing, "and red peppers and citron."

He must have got them from the wealthy man who had the big glass hothouse in town. Things almost as fanciful as orange seeds.

"You never know," he said. "They might grow here."

Mark could not speak. But his face must have shown the bright amazement that raced behind it, or else what Joseph said next would never have broken out.

"You don't think I'da made you go for them cows if I'd a knowed you was gonna get hurt, do you?" he said. Almost savagely. "I wouldn'ta cared if they'd a never given another drop o' milk as long as they lived!"

Mark gave him a crazy answer, but it didn't seem crazy to either of them then, because of a sudden something seemed to bridge all the gaps of speech.

"You jumped right over the bars when you saw I was hurt, didn't you!" he said. "You never even took the top one down. You just jumped right clear over em!"

His father turned his face away, and it looked as if his shoulders were taking a long deep breath.

Joseph let him walk back to the house.

When they went to the kitchen, Mark's sister said, "Where did you go?"

For no reason he could explain Mark felt another sudden compact with his father, that this should be some sort of secret.

"Just out," he said.

"Just out around," Joseph echoed.

And Mark knew that never again would he have to...shift...himself at the sound of his father's footsteps. Not ever.

How do you suppose the "opposing forces" between father and son developed?

If you could write a letter to Mark or his father, what would you say?

What future do you predict for Mark? What makes you think so?

The Snow Woman

BY NORAH BURKE

As she looked, Lha-mo thought she glimpsed something moving, a tall white figure, sometimes upright and sometimes down like an animal.

One morning Lha-mo found the tracks of a snow man and followed them.

Normally she would have been far too frightened to do so, but this time there was a compelling reason.

She stood dumbfounded, staring at that mark of a naked foot in the drift. The prints were large and fresh, but filling up fast with falling snow.

This was not the first time Lha-mo had seen the trail of a yeti, for all her life had been lived here in the high Himalayas, and she had grown up with the knowledge that among these thousands of kilometres of snow there lived a great creature unknown to the rest of the world. But such prints were rare, and these were nearly as fresh as her own.

Lha-mo was a Bhutia woman, always smiling. The piercing climate had made her people squat and sturdy. She too. She stood now, a little dumpy figure in a vast landscape. Alone among giant peaks, in the snow, under the lowering sky, she was a bundle of old but handsome and workmanlike clothes. Snow-roses glowed in her brown cheeks. There was a knife in her belt, and her heart was strong.

She looked up now, after the tracks which continued steadily over the snowfield and up some scree and along a ridge and—

She was already far from home, having come to search for some strayed animals. Her husband and all her brothers-in-law were out too. There was no one left behind in the yak-hair tents except her little son and his grandmother.

Lha-mo smiled, thinking of him, her jewel. How he had yelled when he realized that his mother was going out and that he was to be left behind! How he had clung to her, burying his face in her clothing and drawing the cloth over his ears, to shut out unpleasant things.

He, like Lha-mo, had been born into this life of tents and herds, and movement from place to place, as they pastured their animals or traded in salt and borax, in musk, wool, yak tails, herbs, and such; and just now they were crossing this high range, on their way to other valleys.

Once a year, the nomads descended from their steppes and snows into the little raggle-taggle towns to sell and to buy.

It was there that Lha-mo had heard about the expedition come from Darjeeling into these mountains to search for the yeti. It was there that she had seen white faces for the first time in her life, and been told of the huge rewards which were on offer for news of tracks, for descriptions of the animal, bits of skin, anything.

And it was there that she had seen the necklace!

Kokh Bazaar was one of the last villages for climbers on their way to Everest and other peaks; and this new scientific expedition was making the place its headquarters, from which mobile units could dart out with camera and rifle after information of any kind.

"These madmen," smiled Kokh Bazaar, "they do not believe the yeti exists, but they have come to look for it! Imagine!"

But the foreigners said: "The tracks could be those of a bear or of a langur monkey. Any marks a day or two old become larger as they melt under strong sun. Such prints may be made sometimes by one creature, sometimes another, which would account for the conflicting descriptions of them. Some four-footed animals place the hind foot in the print of the front one, thus giving the impression of a two-footed upright being."

As Lha-mo and her people had moved about in the stinking bazaar—filth protects from cold—she had heard all the talk.

She saw pomegranates and water melons laid out for sale, and guns being made. She examined beads and cloth.

The silversmith sat in front of his open shop, making a necklace. Turquoise, amber, and coral were being put into silver, and he was using prodigious quantities of all these things.

It was no ordinary necklace. Up till that moment, Lha-mo had been perfectly content—even proud—with her own numerous ornaments, but now she saw that they were only thin silver hoops. This necklace that was being made to some lady's order was broad, new, and splendid, unlike anything she'd ever imagined. In the sun it flashed, not extinguished by the grime of wear. The intricacies of the silver were not filled level with black dirt. The necklace was not for sale, but it could be copied.

She had thought of the thing ever since, and now here were yeti tracks—

Her heart began to pound.

All that she had ever heard about the beast came back to her.

"It is fierce. It eats people. To meet one is to die. It is unlucky even to come upon the tracks. Whenever you see them, Lha-mo, run away!"

But now she made up her mind to follow, and alone. There was no time to fetch anyone else. Snow was covering the tracks fast, and she was already a long way from camp. If this trail was to be followed, to discover the gorge or cave where the creature lived, it must be now, at once. When she had pinpointed the area, she could return with others to kill the beast, or capture it.

After all, the rewards were great. Besides the necklace, there would be splendid clothes for all the family. Much food. She could see already a blue satin cap, stitched with gold thread, for the boy. Next year when they went down into the warm valleys, they would buy apricots and peaches, and boxes made of poplar or walnut in which to store their wealth. There would be something more to eat than meat and tea and barley. Already she could taste pink apricot juice on her tongue. She saw her whole family warmed by food and good fortune.

There were all these reasons, but the necklace sparkled clearest of all. She listened.

Wind and snow whispered together. She heard the long singing crack of ice. She heard her own breath and heart. Nothing else.

Her knife was a fine one, kept sharp, to flay meat and shape leather. It had a rough turquoise in the hilt, and enamel. Now she whetted it on a stone till the sound quavered on the glassy air.

The footprints had toes, and so she hesitated, wondering which way to go, because it is known that the yeti's toes are on the back of its feet.

But a glance at the tracks convinced her that this could not be so. The pressure and the drag indicated that the creature was going the other way.

Tibetan women are independent and resolute; Lha-mo was as bold as any, and impulsive too. She decided to rely on her lifelong knowledge of tracks and follow forward as she would have done for any other animal.

She set out, leaning into the driving snow.

It was second nature to her to notice landmarks as she went, and thus remember the way back; so she had no fear of losing herself, however far she might go.

The air was so cold that her breath not only smoked but seemed as if it must drop in ice. Yet she herself, fortified by all the cups of buttered tea which she had already drunk this morning, and for which she carried always the ingredients in the blousing of her clothes, so that no weather would catch her out without it—she herself was so hot, she steamed, and had to open her clothing to let the cruel air cool her skin.

Flakes whirled, the sky was full, and all the world was lit by the dark light of snow.

Although the yeti tracks were disappearing, they were easy to follow.

"It is taller than I am," she thought, "and heavier."

Now and then Lha-mo stopped to see if the wind could tell her anything. Scent of any kind means life, but up here no resin or animals altered the thin air. Each lungful was the purest in the world. Although she did see the lollop of hare-tracks in the snow, and once a flick of black and red—a chough hopping among rocks—she was almost above life now.

Several kilometres of snow-desert lay between her and the smoky smelly tents of home, where her little son waited to burrow his face against her, in shy joy at her return.

She settled into a steady plod that took her across drifts and packed snow, over swept rock and ice, and glacier and moraine, up and down steep slopes; and still the tracks chained on and on into unknown country.

Snow squeaked underfoot. There was the brush-brush of her own clothes. Otherwise only the wind. Once she broke through a snow-crust on to rock and jarred her spine.

But look! Here the creature had stopped by the wayside. And here snow was still melted where it had sat down. Steppe grasses were showing through. Lha-mo knelt and sniffed. There was scent, but nothing she recognized. An unknown animal.

She got up, brushing her knees, and gazed ahead, her heart going. In front rose an escarpment, broken by gullies. Was it time to turn back? Was this the place?

Even as she looked, she thought she glimpsed something moving, a tall white figure, sometimes upright and sometimes down like an animal; but next minute she rubbed the snow mirages from her eyes and saw that there was nothing.

She walked on.

The tracks went forward into a narrow ravine and Lha-mo halted.

In the gorge a pebble rattled.

It would be mad to enter such a place. Instead, she climbed swiftly and silently onto the ridge alongside, then wriggled to the knife-edge to look down into the gully below.

For a moment there was nothing. Then movement showed up a live thing. Almost directly below her and unaware of her presence was an animal she had never seen before. Was it a bear or ape? She had no idea. She could see only that it was large, and for a moment she took it to be white. Then the wind, blowing from behind, lifted the floppy silver gloss of topcoat, and she saw that underneath the white was cinnamon. If this animal took to living lower down, it would turn brown.

Ah, if only she had got with her one of those beautiful guns from Kokh Bazaar, she could have killed and skinned this treasure, and gone home with triumph, with the the pelt folded on her back and edged with red icicles. The chance of a lifetime was here at hand, never to come again.

A weapon?

Beside her lay a big boulder.

Lha-mo got her shoulder against it, and at the third heave she pushed it over the edge.

The boulder whistled down on to the yeti. The animal leaped for safety, but too late. The rock took it on the head, and rock and animal rolled together to the bottom of the defile where the yeti lay motionless. Echoes went ringing everywhere, and setting off avalanches.

Lha-mo, glittering with success, waited for the commotion to be over. Then, as the animal did not move, she drew her knife and scrambled down after it.

There it lay, among snow and pebbles, a mound of heavy silvery hair, much bigger than she had expected from above. She threw one or two stones at it first, to make sure it was dead.

When it still did not move, she approached, but as she got nearer, she saw that it was breathing.

Stunned perhaps?

She sprinted to finish it off with her knife before it regained consciousness.

But it was not a snow man. It was a snow woman with a baby.

The baby was unhurt. He was about the size of a human baby. Her own, for instance. And as she raced up to them, he gave a cry and buried his face against his mother, drawing her long fur over his ears.

Lha-mo recoiled as if shot.

She gasped a horrified breath into her.

Then she backed out, and turned and ran.

That rich mad expedition would now go home and tell the world that there was no such thing as a yeti, and that all the hill people were ignorant and superstitious, but she did not care.

Before she was out of sight, she looked back. The yeti was rising and shaking her head. She picked up her child and bounded away.

Lha-mo made for home as fast as ever she could. As she approached it, she saw that the strayed animals were back, rounded up by one of the others, no doubt. She went in and sat down by the fire, and began to shake.

She was late, of course, and her husband angry.

"Where have you been?" he demanded.

"Out," replied Lha-mo.

———

Did Lha-mo make the right decision? What would you have done in her place?

Can you recall an important but difficult decision you had to make? How did it feel? Would you make the same decision today?

If you were to make a film of this story, would you add dialogue?

ACKNOWLEDGEMENTS

The publishers have made every effort to trace the source of materials appearing in this book. Information that will enable the publishers to rectify any error or omission will be welcomed.

"Future Tense," by Robert Lipsyte from *Sixteen Short Stories by Outstanding Writers for Young Adults* edited by Donald R. Gallo. "Future Tense" copyright © 1984 by Robert Lipsyte. Reprinted by permission of Delacorte Press, a division of Bantam, Doubleday, Dell Publishing Group, Inc.

"The Monkey's Paw," by W.W. Jacobs, reprinted by permission of The Society of Authors as the literary representative of the Estate of W.W. Jacobs.

"Nothing Happens on the Moon," by Paul Ernst, copyright 1939 by Street & Smith Publications, Inc. First appeared in *Street & Smith's Astounding Science Fiction*. Reprinted by permission of Davis Publications, Inc.

"The Old Man," by Holloway Horn from *Travelers in Time: Strange Tales of Man's Journeying into the Past and the Future*, edited by P. Van D. Stern. Published by Doubleday, 1947.

"Hobbyist," by Frederic Brown, reprinted by permission of the author and the author's agents, Scott Meredith Literary Agency, Inc., 845 Third Avenue, New York, New York 10022.

"All the Years of Her Life," by Morley Callaghan. Copyright 1936, 1962. Reprinted by permission of Macmillan of Canada, A Division of Canada Publishing Corporation.

"The Cat," by Nick Mitchell, from *Puzzle: A Multicultural Anthology for Young Readers*, Winnipeg: Peguis Publishers Ltd., 1986. Reprinted with permission.

"Goalie," by Rudy Thauberger from *The Rocket, the Flower, the Hammer and Me* (Polestar Press, 1988), copyright by Rudy Thauberger and reprinted by permission of the author.

"The Good Provider," by Marion Gross from *Science Fiction Adventures in Dimension*, edited by G. Conklin. Published by Vanguard Publishers, 1953.

"G. Trueheart, Man's Best Friend," by James McNamee from *Over the Horizon and Around the World in Fifteen Stories*. Reprinted by permission of Victor Gollancz Ltd.

"Golden Pants," by Roger Lemelin. Translated by Philip Stratford. Reprinted by permission of the author.

"The Crystal Stars Have Just Begun to Shine," by Martha Brooks, reprinted from *Paradise Café and Other Stories* (Thistledown Press, 1988) with permission.

"Maelstrom II," by Arthur C. Clarke, reprinted by permission of the author and the author's agents, Scott Meredith Literary Agency, Inc., 845 Third Avenue, New York, New York 10022.

"Uneasy Home-coming," by Will F. Jenkins, reprinted by permission of the author and the author's agents, Scott Meredith Literary Agency, Inc., 845 Third Avenue, New York, New York 10022.

PHOTOGRAPHS

ILLUSTRATIONS

PRINTED IN CANADA